NORDIC TALES

NORDIC TALES

FOLKTALES FROM
*Norway, Sweden, Finland,
Iceland, and Denmark*

ILLUSTRATIONS BY
Ulla Thynell

CHRONICLE BOOKS
SAN FRANCISCO

Library of Congress Cataloging-in-Publication Data available.

ISBN 978-1-4521-7447-1

Manufactured in China.

20 19 18 17 16 15 14 13 12 11

Design by Maggie Edelman.

Illustrations by Ulla Thynell.

Chronicle books and gifts are available at special quantity discounts to corporations, professional associations, literacy programs, and other organizations. For details and discount information, please contact our premiums department at corporatesales@chroniclebooks.com or at 1-800-759-0190.

Chronicle Books LLC
680 Second Street
San Francisco, California 94107
www.chroniclebooks.com

꒰◆꒱

"When he had finished his story everyone was silent for wonder,
except Hildur, who went up to him and said:
'I declare you to be a liar in all that you have said, unless
you can prove it by sure evidence.'"

–JÓN ARNASON, TRANSLATED BY
GEORGE E. J. POWELL AND EIRÍKUR MAGNÚSSON,
"Hildur, the Queen of the Elves"

꒰◆꒱

CONTENTS

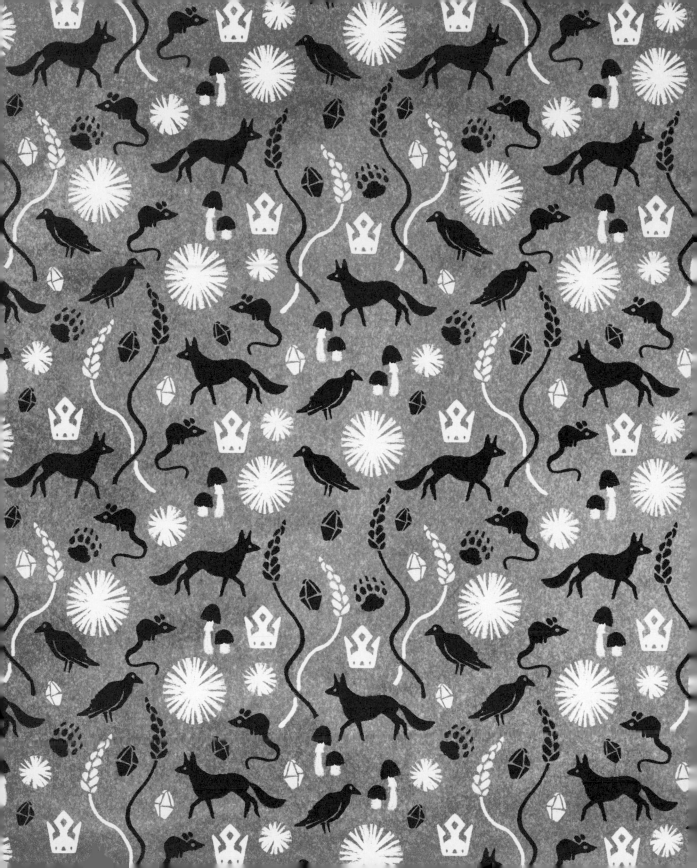

TRANSFORMATION

THE FOREST BRIDE:
THE STORY
of a LITTLE MOUSE
WHO WAS a PRINCESS

Finland

There was once a farmer who had three sons. One day when the boys were grown to manhood he said to them: "My sons, it is high time that you were all married. To-morrow I wish you to go out in search of brides."

"But where shall we go?" the oldest son asked.

"I have thought of that, too," the father said. "Do each of you chop down a tree and then take the direction in which the fallen tree points. I'm sure that each of you if you go far enough in that direction will find a suitable bride."

So the next day the three sons chopped down trees. The oldest son's tree fell pointing north. "That suits me!" he said, for he knew that to the north lay a farm where a very pretty girl lived.

The tree of the second son when it fell pointed south. "That suits me!" the second son declared thinking of a girl that he had often danced with who lived on a farm to the south.

The youngest son's tree—the youngest son's name was Veikko—when it fell pointed straight to the forest.

"Ha! Ha!" the older brothers laughed. "Veikko will have to go courting one of the Wolf girls or one of the Foxes!"

They meant by this that only animals lived in the forest and they thought they were making a good joke at Veikko's expense. But Veikko said he was perfectly willing to take his chances and go where his tree pointed.

The older brothers went gaily off and presented their suits to the two farmers whose daughters they admired. Veikko, too, started off with brave front but after he had gone some distance in the forest his courage began to ebb.

"How can I find a bride," he asked himself, "in a place where there are no human creatures at all!"

Just then he came to a little hut. He pushed open the door and went in. It was empty. To be sure there was a little mouse sitting on the table, daintily combing her whiskers, but a mouse of course doesn't count.

"There's nobody here!" Veikko said aloud.

The little mouse paused in her toilet and turning towards him said reproachfully: "Why, Veikko, I'm here!"

"But you don't count. You're only a mouse!"

"Of course I count!" the little mouse declared. "But tell me, what were you hoping to find?"

"I was hoping to find a sweetheart."

The little mouse questioned him further and Veikko told her the whole story of his brothers and the trees.

"The two older ones are finding sweethearts easily enough," Veikko said, "but I don't see how I can off here in the forest. And it will shame me to have to go home and confess that I alone have failed."

"See here, Veikko," the little mouse said, "why don't you take me for your sweetheart?"

Veikko laughed heartily. "But you're only a mouse! Whoever heard of a man having a mouse for a sweetheart!"

The mouse shook her little head solemnly. "Take my word for it, Veikko, you could do much worse than have me for a sweetheart! Even if I am only a mouse I can love you and be true to you."

She was a dear dainty little mouse and as she sat looking up at Veikko with her little paws under her chin and her bright little eyes sparkling Veikko liked her more and more.

Then she sang Veikko a pretty little song and the song cheered him so much that he forgot his disappointment at not finding a human sweetheart and as he left her to go home he said:

"Very well, little mouse, I'll take you for my sweetheart!"

At that the mouse made little squeaks of delight and she told him that she'd be true to him and wait for him no matter how long he was in returning.

Well, the older brothers when they got home boasted loudly about their sweethearts.

"Mine," said the oldest, "has the rosiest reddest cheeks you ever saw!"

"And mine," the second announced, "has long yellow hair!"

Veikko said nothing.

"What's the matter, Veikko?" the older brothers asked him, laughing. "Has your sweetheart pretty pointed ears or sharp white teeth?"

You see they were still having their little joke about foxes and wolves.

"You needn't laugh," Veikko said. "I've found a sweetheart. She's a gentle dainty little thing gowned in velvet."

"Gowned in velvet!" echoed the oldest brother with a frown.

"Just like a princess!" the second brother sneered.

"Yes," Veikko repeated, "gowned in velvet like a princess. And when she sits up and sings to me I'm perfectly happy."

"Huh!" grunted the older brothers not at all pleased that Veikko should have so grand a sweetheart.

"Well," said the old farmer after a few days, "now I should like to know what those sweethearts of yours are able to do. Have them each bake me a loaf of bread so that I can see whether they're good housewives."

"Mine will be able to bake bread—I'm sure of that!" the oldest brother declared boastfully.

"So will mine!" chorused the second brother.

Veikko was silent.

"What about the Princess?" they said with a laugh. "Do you think the Princess can bake bread?"

"I don't know," Veikko answered truthfully. "I'll have to ask her."

Of course he had no reason for supposing that the little mouse could bake bread and by the time he reached the hut in the forest he was feeling sad and discouraged.

When he pushed open the door he found the little mouse as before seated on the table daintily combing her whiskers. At the sight of Veikko she danced about with delight.

"I'm so glad to see you!" she squeaked. "I knew you would come back!"

Then when she noticed that he was silent she asked him what was the matter. Veikko told her:

"My father wants each of our sweethearts to bake him a loaf of bread. If I come home without a loaf my brothers will laugh at me."

"You won't have to go home without a loaf!" the little mouse said. "I can bake bread."

Veikko was much surprised at this.

"I never heard of a mouse that could bake bread!"

"Well, I can!" the little mouse insisted.

With that she began ringing a small silver bell, *tinkle, tinkle, tinkle.* Instantly there was the sound of hurrying footsteps, tiny scratchy footsteps, and hundreds of mice came running into the hut.

The little Princess mouse sitting up very straight and dignified said to them:

"Each of you go fetch me a grain of the finest wheat."

All the mice scampered quickly away and soon returned one by one, each carrying a grain of the finest wheat. After that it was no trick at all for the Princess mouse to bake a beautiful loaf of wheaten bread.

The next day the three brothers presented their father the loaves of their sweethearts' baking. The oldest one had a loaf of rye bread.

"Very good," the farmer said. "For hardworking people like us rye bread is good."

The loaf the second son had was made of barley.

"Barley bread is also good," the farmer said.

But when Veikko presented his loaf of beautiful wheaten bread, his father cried out:

"What! White bread! Ah, Veikko now must have a sweetheart of wealth!"

"Of course!" the older brothers sneered. "Didn't he tell us she was a Princess? Say, Veikko, when a Princess wants fine white flour, how does she get it?"

Veikko answered simply:

"She rings a little silver bell and when her servants come in she tells them to bring her grains of the finest wheat."

At this the older brothers nearly exploded with envy until their father had to reprove them.

"There! There!" he said. "Don't grudge the boy his good luck! Each girl has baked the loaf she knows how to make and each in her own way will probably make a good wife. But before you bring them home to me I want one further test of their skill in housewifery. Let them each send me a sample of their weaving."

The older brothers were delighted at this for they knew that their sweethearts were skilful weavers.

"We'll see how her ladyship fares this time!" they said, sure in their hearts that Veikko's sweetheart, whoever she was, would not put them to shame with her weaving.

Veikko, too, had serious doubts of the little mouse's ability at the loom.

"Whoever heard of a mouse that could weave?" he said to himself as he pushed open the door of the forest hut.

"Oh, there you are at last!" the little mouse squeaked joyfully.

She reached out her little paws in welcome and then in her excitement she began dancing about on the table.

"Are you really glad to see me, little mouse?" Veikko asked.

"Indeed I am!" the mouse declared. "Am I not your sweetheart? I've been waiting for you and waiting, just wishing that you would return! Does your father want something more this time, Veikko?"

"Yes, and it's something I'm afraid you can't give me, little mouse."

"Perhaps I can. Tell me what it is."

"It's a sample of your weaving. I don't believe you can weave. I never heard of a mouse that could weave."

"Tut! Tut!" said the mouse. "Of course I can weave! It would be a strange thing if Veikko's sweetheart couldn't weave!"

She rang the little silver bell, *tinkle, tinkle, tinkle,* and instantly there was the faint *scratch-scratch* of a hundred little feet as mice came running in from all directions and sat up on their haunches awaiting their Princess' orders.

"Go each of you," she said, "and get me a fiber of flax, the finest there is."

The mice went scurrying off and soon they began returning one by one each bringing a fiber of flax. When they had spun the flax and carded it, the little mouse wove a beautiful piece of fine linen. It was so sheer that she was able when she folded it to put it into an empty nutshell.

"Here, Veikko," she said, "here in this little box is a sample of my weaving. I hope your father will like it."

Veikko when he got home felt almost embarrassed for he was sure that his sweetheart's weaving would shame his brothers. So at first he kept the nutshell hidden in his pocket.

The sweetheart of the oldest brother had sent as a sample of her weaving a square of coarse cotton.

"Not very fine," the farmer said, "but good enough."

The second brother's sample was a square of cotton and linen mixed.

"A little better," the farmer said, nodding his head.

Then he turned to Veikko.

"And you, Veikko, has your sweetheart not given you a sample of her weaving?"

Veikko handed his father a nutshell at sight of which his brothers burst out laughing.

"Ha! Ha! Ha!" they laughed. "Veikko's sweetheart gives him a nut when he asks for a sample of her weaving."

But their laughter died as the farmer opened the nutshell and began shaking out a great web of the finest linen.

"Why, Veikko, my boy!" he cried, "however did your sweetheart get threads for so fine a web?"

Veikko answered modestly:

"She rang a little silver bell and ordered her servants to bring her in fibers of finest flax. They did so and after they had spun the flax and carded it, my sweetheart wove the web you see."

"Wonderful!" gasped the farmer. "I have never known such a weaver! The other girls will be all right for farmers' wives but Veikko's sweetheart might be a Princess! Well," concluded the farmer, "it's time that you all brought your sweethearts home. I want to see them with my own eyes. Suppose you bring them to-morrow."

"She's a good little mouse and I'm very fond of her," Veikko thought to himself as he went out to the forest, "but my brothers will certainly laugh when they find she is only a mouse! Well, I don't care if they do laugh! She's been a good little sweetheart to me and I'm not going to be ashamed of her!"

So when he got to the hut he told the little mouse at once that his father wanted to see her.

The little mouse was greatly excited.

"I must go in proper style!" she said.

She rang the little silver bell and ordered her coach and five. The coach when it came turned out to be an empty nutshell and the five prancing steeds that were drawing it were five black mice. The little mouse seated herself in the coach with a coachman mouse on the box in front of her and a footman mouse on the box behind her.

"Oh, how my brothers will laugh!" thought Veikko.

But he didn't laugh. He walked beside the coach and told the little mouse not to be frightened, that he would take good care of her. His father, he told her, was a gentle old man and would be kind to her.

When they left the forest they came to a river which was spanned by a foot bridge. Just as Veikko and the nutshell coach had reached the middle of the bridge, a man met them coming from the opposite direction.

"Mercy me!" the man exclaimed as he caught sight of the strange little coach that was rolling along beside Veikko. "What's that?"

He stooped down and looked and then with a loud laugh he put out his foot and pushed the coach, the little mouse, her servants, and her five prancing steeds—all off the bridge and into the water below.

"What have you done! What have you done!" Veikko cried. "You've drowned my poor little sweetheart!"

The man thinking Veikko was crazy hurried away.

Veikko with tears in his eyes looked down into the water.

"You poor little mouse!" he said. "How sorry I am that you are drowned! You were a faithful loving sweetheart and now that you are gone I know how much I loved you!"

As he spoke he saw a beautiful coach of gold drawn by five glossy horses go up the far bank of the river. A coachman in gold lace held the reins and a footman in pointed cap sat up stiffly behind. The most beautiful girl in the world was seated in the coach. Her skin was as red as a berry and as white as snow, her long golden hair gleamed with jewels, and she was dressed in pearly velvet. She beckoned to Veikko and when he came close she said:

"Won't you come sit beside me?"

"Me? Me?" Veikko stammered, too dazed to think.

The beautiful creature smiled.

"You were not ashamed to have me for a sweetheart when I was a mouse," she said, "and surely now that I am a Princess again you won't desert me!"

"A mouse!" Veikko gasped. "Were you the little mouse?"

The Princess nodded.

"Yes, I was the little mouse under an evil enchantment which could never have been broken if you had not taken me for a sweetheart and if another human being had not drowned me. Now the enchantment is broken forever. So come, we will go to your father and after he has given us his blessing we will get married and go home to my kingdom."

And that's exactly what they did. They drove at once to the farmer's house and when Veikko's father and his brothers and his brothers' sweethearts saw the Princess' coach stopping at their gate they all came out bowing and scraping to see what such grand folk could want of them.

"Father!" Veikko cried, "don't you know me?"

The farmer stopped bowing long enough to look up.

"Why, bless my soul!" he cried, "it's our Veikko!"

"Yes, father, I'm Veikko and this is the Princess that I'm going to marry!"

"A Princess, did you say, Veikko? Mercy me, where did my boy find a Princess?"

"Out in the forest where my tree pointed."

"Well, well, well," the farmer said, "where your tree pointed! I've always heard that was a good way to find a bride."

The older brothers shook their heads gloomily and muttered:

"Just our luck! If only our trees had pointed to the forest we, too, should have found princesses instead of plain country wenches!"

But they were wrong: it wasn't because his tree pointed to the forest that Veikko got the Princess, it was because he was so simple and good that he was kind even to a little mouse.

Well, after they had got the farmer's blessing they rode home to the Princess' kingdom and were married. And they were happy as they should have been for they were good and true to each other and they loved each other dearly.

EAST of the SUN
and WEST of the MOON

Norway

There was once a poor tenant who had many children, but very little food or clothes to give them; they were all pretty children, but the prettiest was the youngest daughter, who was so lovely that there was almost too much of her loveliness.

So one Thursday evening, late in the autumn, when there was terrible weather and it was dreadfully dark out of doors, and it rained and blew as well till the wall creaked, they were all sitting by the hearth busy with something or other. All at once some one knocked three times on the window-pane. The goodman went out to see what was the matter; when he came outside he saw a great big white bear.

"Good evening!" said the white bear. —"Good evening!" said the man.—"Will you give me your youngest daughter, and I will make you as rich as you now are poor," said the bear.—Yes; the man thought it would be very nice to be so rich, but he must speak with his daughter first; so he went in and told her that a great white bear was outside, who promised that he would make them rich if he could only get her. She said "No," and would not agree to any such arrangement; so the man went out and arranged with the white bear that he should come again next Thursday evening for an answer. In the meantime they talked her round, and told her of all the riches they would come in possession of, and how fine she herself would have it in her new home; so at last she gave in to their entreaties and began washing and mending her few rags and made herself look as well as she could, and was at last ready for the journey. Her baggage, of course, was not much to speak of.

Next Thursday evening the white bear came to fetch her; she got up on his back with her bundle, and away they went. When they had gone some distance the white bear said: "Are you afraid?"—No, she wasn't afraid.—"Well, only hold tight by my coat and there's no danger," said the bear.

And so she rode far, far away, and came at last to a big mountain. The white bear knocked at it and a gate was opened, and they came into a castle where there were a great many rooms all lit up and gleaming with silver and gold, and amongst these was a great hall, where a table stood ready laid; in fact, all was so grand and splendid that you would not believe it unless you saw it. So the white bear gave her a silver bell, which she was to ring when-ever there was anything she wanted, and her wishes would be attended to at once.

Well, when she had eaten, it was getting late in the evening, and she became sleepy after the journey, so she thought she would like to go to bed. She rang the bell, and had scarcely touched it, before she was in a room, where she found such a beautiful bed as any one could wish for, with silken pillows and curtains, and gold fringes; everything else in the room was made of gold and silver. But when she had gone to bed and put out the light, she heard some one coming into the room and sitting down in the big arm-chair near the bed. It was the white bear, who at night could throw off his shape, and she could hear by his snoring as he sat in the chair that he was now in the shape of a man; but she never saw him, because he always came after she had put out the light, and in the morning before the day dawned he was gone.

Well, for a while everything went on happily, but then she began to be silent and sorrowful, for she went about all day alone, and no wonder she longed to be home with her parents and her sisters and brothers again. When the white bear asked what ailed her, she said she was so lonely there, she walked about all alone, and longed for her home and her parents and brothers and sisters, and that was the reason she was so sad.

"But you may visit them, if you like," said the white bear, "if you will only promise me one thing. You must never talk alone with your mother, but only when there are others in the room. She will take you by the hand and try to lead you into a room to speak with you all by yourself; but you must not do this by any means, or you will make us both unhappy, and bring misfortune over us."

One Sunday the white bear came and told her that they were now going to see her parents. Away they went, she sitting on his back, and they travelled far and long; at last they came to a grand white farmhouse, where her sisters and brothers were running about. Everything was so pretty that it was a pleasure to see it.

"Your parents are living there," said the bear; "but mind you don't forget what I have said, or you will make us both unhappy." No, she would not forget it. When they came to the farm, the bear turned round and went away.

There was such a joy when she came in to her parents that there was no end to it. They said they did not know how to thank her fully for what she had done for them. They had everything they wanted, and everybody asked after her and wanted to know how she was getting on, and where she was living. She said that she was very comfortable and had everything she wished for; but what she other-wise answered I don't know, but I believe they did not get much out of her.

But one day after dinner it happened exactly as the white bear had said; her mother wanted to speak with her alone in her chamber. But she recollected what the bear had told her, and would not go with her. "What we have got to talk about, we can do at some other time," she said. But somehow or other her mother talked her round at last, and so she had to tell her everything. She told her how a man came into her room every night as soon as she had put out the light, and how she never saw him, for he was always gone before the day dawned. She was sorrowful at this, for she thought she would so like to see him; and in the daytime she walked about there all alone and felt very lonely and sad.

"Oh, dear me!" said her mother, "it may be a troll for all we know! But I will tell you how you can get a sight of him. You shall have a piece of a candle from me, and this you must take with you home in your bosom. When he is asleep, light that candle, but take care not to drop any of the tallow on him."—Yes, she took the candle and hid it in her bosom, and in the evening the white bear came and fetched her.

When they had gone some distance of the way the bear asked her if everything hadn't happened as he had said. Yes, she couldn't deny that.—"Well, if you have listened to your mother's advice you will make us both unhappy, and all will be over between us," said the bear.—No, that she hadn't!

When she came home and had gone to bed, the same thing occurred as before. Some one came into the room and sat in the arm-chair by her bedside, but in the middle of the night when she heard that he was asleep, she got up and struck a light, lit the candle, and let the light fall on him. She then saw that he was the loveliest prince any one could wish to see, and she fell at once in love with him; she thought that if she could not kiss him there and then she would not be able to live. And so she did, but she dropped three hot drops of tallow on him, and he woke up.

"What have you done?" he said, "you have now made us both unhappy forever, for if you had only held out one year I should have been saved. I have a stepmother who has bewitched me, and I am now a white bear by day and a man by night. But now all is over between us, and I must leave you and go back to her; she lives in a castle which lies east of the sun and west of the moon, and in the same castle there is a princess with a nose two yards long, and now I must marry her."

She wept and cried, but there was no help for it; he must go and leave her. So she asked him if she might not go with him. No, that was impossible!—"But if you will tell me the way, I will try and find you," she said. "I suppose I may have leave to do that!"—Yes, she could do that, he said, but there was no road to that place; it lay east of the sun and west of the moon, and she could never find her way there.

Next morning when she awoke, both the prince and the castle were gone; she lay on a little green field far in the middle of the dark thick forest, and by her side lay the same bundle with her old rags which she had brought with her from home. When she had rubbed the sleep out of her eyes and wept till she was tired, she set out on her way and walked for many, many a day, till she at last came to a big mountain.

Close to it an old woman sat and played with a golden apple. She asked her if she knew the way to the prince who lived with his stepmother in a castle that lay east of the sun and west of the moon, and who was going to marry a princess with a nose two yards long.—"How do you know him?" asked the old woman, "perhaps it was you who should have had him?"—Yes, it was she. "Ah, indeed! is that you?" said the woman; "well, all I know is that he lives in that castle which lies east of the sun and west of the moon, and thither you will come late or never, but I will lend you my horse, and on him you can ride to my neighbour, an old friend of mine;

perhaps she can tell you. When you have got there, just give my horse a blow with your whip under the left ear and ask him to go home again;—and you had better take this golden apple with you."

So she got up on the horse and rode a long, long time till she at last came to a mountain, where an old woman was sitting with a golden carding-comb. She asked her if she knew the way to the castle which lay east of the sun and west of the moon. She answered like the first old woman, that she didn't know anything about it, but it was sure to be east of the sun and west of the moon, "and thither you will come, early or late, but I will lend you my horse as far as my neighbour; perhaps she can tell you. When you have got there, just give my horse a blow under the left ear and ask him to go home again." And the old woman gave her the golden carding-comb, which might come in useful for her.

The young girl got up on the horse and rode for a long, long weary time, and came at last to a large mountain, where an old woman was sitting and spinning on a golden spinning-wheel. She asked her if she knew the way to the prince, and where the castle was that lay east of the sun and west of the moon. And so came the same question: "Perhaps it is you who should have had the prince?"—Yes, it was! But the old woman knew the way no better than the other two. It was east of the sun and west of the moon,—she knew that,—"and thither you will come, early or late," she said, "but I will lend you my horse, and then I think you had better ride to the east wind and ask him. Perhaps he is known about those parts and can blow you there. When you have got there, just touch the horse under the ear and he'll go home again." And so she gave her the golden spinning-wheel. "You might find use for it," said the old woman.

She rode on many days for a long weary time before she got to the east wind, but after a long time she did reach it, and so she asked him if he could tell her the way to the prince, who lived east of the sun and west of the moon. Yes, he had heard tell of that prince, said the east wind, and of the castle too, but he didn't know the way thither, for he had never blown so far. "But if you like, I'll go with you to my brother, the west wind. Perhaps he may know it, for he is much stronger. Just get up on my back and I'll carry you thither."

Yes, she did so, and away they went at a great speed. When they got to the west wind, they went in to him, and the east wind told him that his companion was the one who should have had the prince who lived in the castle, which lay east of the sun and west of the moon; she was now on her way to find him again, and so he had gone with her to hear if the west wind knew where that castle was.—"No, I have never blown so far," said the west wind, "but if you like I'll go with you to the south wind, for he is much stronger than any of us, and he has been far and wide; perhaps he may tell you. You had better sit up on my back and I'll carry you thither."

Well, she got on his back, and off they started for the south wind; they weren't long on the way, I can tell you! When they got there, the west wind asked his brother if he could tell him the way to that castle which lay east of the sun and west of the moon. His companion was the one who should have had the prince who lived there.—"Oh, indeed!" said the south wind, "is that she? Well, I have been to many a nook and corner in my time, but so far I have never blown. But if you like, I'll go with you to my brother, the north wind; he is the oldest and strongest of all of us, and if he doesn't know where it is you will never be able to find any one who can tell you. Just get up on my back and I'll carry you thither."

Yes, she sat up on his back, and away they went at such a rate, that the way didn't seem to be very long.

When they got to where the north wind lived he was so wild and unruly that cold gusts were felt a long way off. "What do you want?" he shouted from far away, but still it made them shiver all over.—"Oh, you needn't be so very harsh," said the south wind, "it's I, your own brother; and then I have got her with me who should have had the prince who lives in that castle which lies east of the sun and west of the moon, and she wants to ask you if you have ever been there and if you can tell her the way. She is so very anxious to find him again."—"Well, yes, I do know where it is," said the north wind; "I once blew an aspen leaf thither, but I was so tired that I wasn't able to blow for many days after. But if you really intend going there and you are not afraid to come with me, I will take you on my back and try if I can blow you so far."—Yes, she was willing; she must go thither, if it were possible, one way or another, and she wasn't a bit afraid, go how it would.

"Very well!" said the north wind, "you must stop here to-night then, for we must have a whole day before us and perhaps more, if we are to reach it."

Early next morning the north wind called her, and then he blew himself out and made himself so big and strong that he was terrible to look at. Away they went, high up through the air at such a fearful speed, as if they were going to the end of the world. There was such a hurricane on land that trees and houses were blown down, and when they came out on the big sea ships were wrecked by hundreds. And onwards they swept, so far, far, that no one would believe how far they went, and still farther and farther out to sea, till the north wind got more and more tired and so knocked up that he was scarcely able to give another blow, and was sinking and going down more and more and at last they were so low that the tops of the billows touched their heels.

"Are you afraid?" said the north wind.—"No," she said, she wasn't a bit afraid. But they were not so very far from land either, and the north wind had just sufficient strength left to reach the shore and put her off just under the windows of the castle which lay east of the sun and west of the moon; but he was then so tired and worn out that he had to rest for many days before he could start on his way home again.

Next morning she sat down under the castle windows, and began playing with the golden apple, and the first one she saw was the princess with the long nose, whom the prince was going to marry.

"What do you want for that golden apple of yours?" she asked and opened the casement.—"It is not for sale, neither for gold nor money," said the girl.—"If it isn't for sale for gold or money, what do you want for it then?" said the princess; "I'll give you what you ask!"—"Well, if I to-night may sit in the arm-chair by the bedside of the prince who lives here, you shall have it," said the girl who came with the north wind.—Yes, she might do that, there would be no difficulty about that.

So the princess got the golden apple; but when the girl came up into the prince's bedroom in the evening, he was fast asleep; she called him and shook him, and now and then she cried and wept; but no, she could not wake him up so that she might speak to him. Next morning, as soon as the day dawned, the princess with the long nose came and turned her out of the room.

Later in the day she sat down under the castle windows and began carding with her golden carding-comb, and then the same thing happened again. The princess asked her what she wanted for the carding-comb, and she told her that it wasn't for sale neither for gold nor money, but if she might get leave to sit in the arm-chair by the prince's bedside that night, she should have it. But when she came up into the bedroom she found him fast asleep again, and for all she cried and shook him, for all she wept, he slept so soundly that she could not get life into him; and when the day dawned in the early morning, in came the princess with the long nose and turned her out of the room again.

So as the day wore on, she sat down under the castle windows and began spinning on the spinning-wheel, and that the princess with the long nose wanted also to have. She opened the casement and asked the girl what she wanted for it. The girl told her, as she had done twice before, that it was not for sale either for gold or money, but if she might sit in the arm-chair by the prince's bedside that night she should have it. Yes, she might do that. But there were some Christian people who had been carried off and were imprisoned in the room next to the prince's, and they had heard that some woman had been in his room and wept and cried and called his name two nights running, and this they told the prince.

In the evening, when the princess came and brought him his drink, he made appear as if he drank, but he threw it over his shoulder, for he felt sure she had put a sleeping draught in his drink.

So when the girl came into his room that night she found the prince wide awake, and then she told him how she had come there. "You have just come in time," said the prince, "for to-morrow I was to be married to the princess; but I won't have that Longnose, and you are the only one that can save me. I will say that I shall want to see what my bride can do, and if she is fit to be my wife; then I will ask her to wash the shirt with the three tallow stains on it. She will try, for she does not know that it is you who dropped the tallow on the shirt; but that can only be done by Christian folks, and not by a pack of trolls like we have in this place; and so I will say that I will not have anybody else for a bride except the one who can wash the shirt clean, and I know you can do that." And they felt very glad and happy, and they went on talking all night about the joyful time in store for them.

The next day, when the wedding was to take place, the prince said: "I think I must see first what my bride can do!"—"Yes, quite so!" said the stepmother. "I have got a very fine shirt, which I am going to use for my wedding shirt; but there are three tallow stains on it which I want washed out; and I have made a vow that I will not take any other woman for a wife than the one who is able to do that; if she cannot do that, she is not worth having," said the prince. "Well, that was easy enough," said the stepmother and agreed to this trial. Well, the princess with the long nose set to washing the best she could, but the more she washed the bigger grew the stains. "Why, you cannot wash," said the old witch, her stepmother; "let me try!"—but no sooner did she take the shirt than it got still worse, and the more she washed and rubbed the bigger and blacker the stains grew.

So did the other trolls try their hands at washing, but the longer they worked at it the dirtier the shirt grew, till at last it looked as if it had been up the chimney. "Ah, you are not worth anything, the whole lot of you!" said the prince; "there's a poor girl under the window just outside here, and I am sure she can wash much better than any of you. Come in, my girl!" he shouted out to her.—Yes, she would come in.—"Can you wash this shirt clean?" asked the prince.—"Well, I don't know," she said, "but I will try."

And no sooner had she taken the shirt and dipped it in the water, than it was as white as the driven snow, if not whiter.

"Yes, you shall be my wife," said the prince. But the old witch flew into such a rage that she burst; and the princess with the long nose and all the trolls must have burst also, for I never heard of them since. The prince and his bride then set free all the people who had been carried off and imprisoned there, and so they took as much gold and silver with them as they could carry, and moved far away from the castle which lay east of the sun and west of the moon.

THE MAGICIAN'S PUPIL

Denmark

There was once a peasant who had a son, whom, when of a proper age, his father apprenticed to a trade; but the boy, who had no inclination for work, always ran home again to his parents; at this the father was much troubled, not knowing what course to pursue. One day he entered a church, where, after repeating the Lord's Prayer, he said: "To what trade shall I apprentice my son? He runs away from every place."

The clerk, who happened at that moment to be standing behind the altar, hearing the peasant utter these words, called out in answer: "Teach him witchcraft; teach him witchcraft!"

The peasant, who did not see the clerk, thought it was our Lord who gave him this advice, and determined upon following it.

The next day he said to his son, that he should go with him, and he would find him a new situation. After walking a good way into the country, they met with a shepherd tending his flock.

"Where are you going to, good man?" inquired the shepherd.

"I am in search of a master, who can teach my son the black art," answered the peasant. "You may soon find him," said the shepherd; "keep straight on and you will come to the greatest wizard that is to be found in all the land." The peasant thanked him for this information, and went on. Soon after, he came to a large forest, in the middle of which stood the wizard's house. He knocked at the door, and asked the Troll-man whether he had any inclination to take a boy as a pupil. "Yes," answered the other; "but not for a less term than four years; and we will make this agreement, that at the end of that time, you shall come, and if you can find your son, he shall belong to you, but should you not be able to discover him, he must remain in my house, and serve me for the rest of his life."

The peasant agreed to these conditions, and returned home alone. At the end of a week he began to look for his son's return; thinking that in this, as in all former cases, he would run away from his master. But he did not come back, and his mother began to cry, and say her husband had not acted rightly in giving their child into the power of the evil one, and that they should never see him more.

After four years had elapsed the peasant set out on a journey to the magician's, according to their agreement. A little before he reached the forest, he met the same shepherd, who instructed him how to act so as to get his son back. "When you get there," said he, "you must at night keep your eyes constantly turned towards the fireplace, and take care not to fall asleep, for then the Troll-man will convey you back to your own house, and afterwards say you did not come at the appointed time. To-morrow you will see three dogs in the yard, eating milk-porridge out of a dish. The middle one is your son, and he is the one you must choose."

The peasant thanked the shepherd for his information, and bade him farewell.

When he entered the house of the magician, everything took place as the shepherd had said. He was conducted into the yard, where he saw three dogs. Two of them were handsome with smooth skins, but the third was lean and looked ill. When the peasant patted the dogs, the two handsome ones growled at him, but the lean one, on the contrary, wagged his tail. "Canst thou now tell me which of these three dogs is thy son?" said the Troll-man; "if so thou canst take him with thee; if not, he belongs to me."

"Well then I will choose the one that appears the most friendly," answered the peasant; "although he looks less handsome than the others." "That is a sensible choice," said the Troll-man; "he knew what he was about who gave thee that advice."

The peasant was then allowed to take his son home with him. So, putting a cord round his neck, he went his way, bewailing that his son was changed into a dog. "Oh! why are you bewailing so?" asked the shepherd as he came out of the forest, "it appears to me you have not been so very unlucky."

When he had gone a little way, the dog said to him: "Now you shall see that my learning has been of some use to me. I will soon change myself into a little tiny dog, and then you must sell me to those who are coming past." The dog did as he said, and became a beautiful little creature. Soon after a carriage came rolling along with some great folks in it. When they saw the beautiful little dog that ran playing along the road, and heard that it was for sale, they bought it of the peasant for a considerable sum, and at the same moment the son changed his father into a hare, which he caused to run across the road, while he was taken up by those who had bought him. When they saw the hare they set the dog after it, and scarcely had they done so, than both hare and dog ran into the wood and disappeared. Now the boy changed himself again, and this time both he and his father assumed human forms. The old man began cutting twigs and his son helped him. When the people in the carriage missed the little dog, they got out to seek after it, and asked the old man and his son if they had seen anything of a little dog that had run away. The boy directed them further into the wood, and he and his father returned home, and lived well on the money they had received by selling the dog.

When all the money was spent, both father and son resolved upon going out again in search of adventures. "Now I will turn myself into a boar," said the youth, "and you must put a cord round my leg and take me to Holsens market for sale; but remember to throw the cord over my right ear at the moment you sell me, and then I shall be home again as soon as you."

The peasant did as his son directed him, and went to market; but he set so high a price on the boar, that no one would buy it, so he continued standing in the market till the afternoon was far advanced. At length there came an old man who bought the boar of him. This was no other than the magician, who, angry that the father had got back his son, had never ceased seeking after them from the time they had left his house. When the peasant had sold his boar he threw the cord over its right ear as the lad had told him, and in the same moment the animal vanished; and when he reached his own door he again saw his son sitting at the table.

They now lived a pleasant merry life until all the money was spent, and then again set out on fresh adventures. This time the son changed himself into a bull, first reminding his father to throw the rope over his right ear as soon as he was sold. At the market he met with the same old man, and soon came to an agreement with him about the price of the bull. While they were drinking a glass together in the alehouse, the father threw the rope over the bull's right horn, and when the magician went to fetch his purchase it had vanished, and the peasant upon reaching home again found his son sitting by his mother at the table. The third time the lad turned himself into a horse, and the magician was again in the market and bought him. "Thou hast already tricked me twice," said he to the peasant; "but it shall not happen again." Before he paid down the money he hired a stable and fastened the horse in, so that it was impossible for the peasant to throw the rein over the animal's right ear. The old man, nevertheless, returned home, in the hope that this time also he should find his son; but he was disappointed, for no lad was there. The magician in the meantime mounted the horse and rode off. He well knew whom he had bought, and determined that the boy should pay with his life the deception he had practised upon him. He led the horse through swamps and pools, and galloped at a pace that, had he long continued it, he must have ridden the animal to death; but the horse was a hard trotter, and the magician being old he at last found he had got his master, and was therefore obliged to ride home.

When he arrived at his house he put a magic bridle on the horse and shut him in a dark stable without giving him anything either to eat or drink. When some time had elapsed, he said to the servant-maid: "Go out and see how the horse is." When the girl came into the stable the metamorphosed boy (who had been the girl's sweetheart while he was in the Troll's house) began to moan piteously, and begged her to give him a pail of water. She did so, and on her return told her master that the horse was well. Some time after he again desired her to go out and see if the horse were not yet dead. When she entered the stable the poor animal begged her to loose the rein and the girths, which were strapped so tight that he could hardly draw breath. The girl did as she was requested, and no sooner was it done than the boy changed himself into a hare and ran out of the stable. The magician, who was sitting in the window, was immediately aware of what had happened on seeing the hare go springing across the yard, and, instantly changing himself into a dog, went in pursuit of it. When they had run many miles over cornfields and meadows, the boy's strength began to fail and the magician gained more and more upon him. The hare then changed itself into a dove, but the magician as quickly turned himself into a hawk and pursued him afresh.

In this manner they flew towards a palace where a princess was sitting at a window. When she saw a hawk in chase of a dove she opened the window, and immediately the dove flew into the room, and then changed itself into a gold ring. The magician now became a prince, and went into the apartment for the purpose of catching the dove. When he could not find it, he asked permission to see her gold rings. The princess showed them to him, but let one fall into the fire. The Troll-man instantly drew it out, in doing which he burnt his fingers, and was obliged to let it fall on the floor. The boy now knew of no better course than to change himself into a grain of corn.

At the same moment the magician became a hen, in order to eat the corn, but scarcely had he done so than the boy became a hawk and killed him.

He then went to the forest, fetched all the magician's gold and silver, and from that day lived in wealth and happiness with his parents.

HILDUR, the QUEEN of the ELVES

ð

Iceland

Once, in a mountainous district, there lived a certain farmer, whose name and that of his farm have not been handed down to us; so we cannot tell them. He was unmarried, and had a housekeeper named Hildur, concerning whose family and descent he knew nothing whatever. She had all the indoor affairs of the farm under her charge, and managed them wondrous well. All the inmates of the house, the farmer himself to boot, were fond of her, as she was clean and thrifty in her habits, and kind and gentle in speech.

Everything about the place flourished exceedingly, but the farmer always found the greatest difficulty in hiring a herdsman; a very important matter, as the well-being of the farm depended not a little on the care taken of the sheep. This difficulty did not arise from any fault of the farmer's own, or from neglect on the part of the housekeeper to the comforts of the servants, but from the fact, that no herdsman who entered his service lived more than a year, each one being without fail found dead in his bed, on the morning of Christmas-day. No wonder, therefore, the farmer found herdsmen scarce.

In those times it was the custom of the country to spend the night of Christmas-eve at church, and this occasion for service was looked upon as a very solemn one. But so far was this farm from the church, that the herdsmen, who did not return from their flocks till late in the evening, were unable to go to it on that night until long after the usual time; and as for Hildur, she always remained behind to take care of the house, and always had so much to do in the way of cleaning the rooms and dealing out the rations for the servants, that the family used to come home from church and go to bed long before she had finished her work, and was able to go to bed herself.

The more the reports of the death of herdsman after herdsman, on the night of Christmas-eve, were spread abroad, the greater became the difficulty the farmer found in hiring one, although it was never supposed for an instant that violence was used towards the men, as no mark had ever been found on their bodies; and as, moreover, there was no one to suspect. At length the farmer declared that his conscience would no longer let him thus hire men only in order that they might die, so he determined in future to let luck take care of his sheep, or the sheep take care of themselves.

Not long after he had made this determination, a bold and hardy-looking man came to him and made him a proffer of his services. The farmer said:

"My good friend, I am not in so great need of your services as to hire you."

Then the man asked him, "Have you, then, taken a herdsman for this winter?"

The farmer said, "No; for I suppose you know what a terrible fate has hitherto befallen every one I have hired."

"I have heard of it," said the other, "but the fear of it shall neither trouble me nor prevent my keeping your sheep this winter for you, if you will but make up your mind to take me."

But the farmer would not hear of it at first; "For," said he, "it is a pity, indeed, that so fine a fellow as you should lose your chance of life. Begone, if you are wise, and get work elsewhere."

Yet still the man declared, again and again, that he cared not a whit for the terrors of Christmas-eve, and still urged the farmer to hire him.

At length the farmer consented, in answer to the man's urgent prayer, to take him as herdsman; and very well they agreed together. For everyone, both high and low, liked the man, as he was honest and open, zealous in everything he laid his hands to, and willing to do anyone a good turn, if need were.

On Christmas-eve, towards nightfall, the farmer and all his family went (as has been before declared to be the custom) to church, except Hildur, who remained behind to look after household matters, and the herdsman, who could not leave his sheep in time. Late in the evening, the latter as usual returned home, and after having eaten his supper, went to bed. As soon as he was well between the sheets, the remembrance struck him of what had befallen all the former herdsmen in his position on the same evening, and he thought it would be the best plan for him to lie awake and thus to be ready for any accident, though he was mighty little troubled with fear. Quite late at night, he heard the farmer and his family return from church, enter the house, and having taken supper, go to bed. Still, nothing happened, except that whenever he closed his eyes for a moment, a strange and deadly faintness stole over him, which only acted as one reason the more for his doing his best to keep awake.

Shortly after he had become aware of these feelings, he heard some one creep stealthily up to the side of his bed, and looking through the gloom at the figure, fancied he recognized Hildur the housekeeper. So he feigned to be fast asleep, and felt her place something in his mouth, which he knew instantly to be the bit of a magic bridle, but yet allowed her to fix it on him, without moving. When she had fastened the bridle, she dragged him from his bed with it, and out of the farmhouse, without his being either able or willing to make the least resistance.

Then mounting on his back, she made him rise from the ground as if on wings, and rode him through the air, till they arrived at a huge and awful precipice, which yawned, like a great well, down into the earth.

She dismounted at a large stone, and fastening the reins to it, leaped into the precipice. But the herdsman, objecting strongly to being tied to this stone all night, and thinking to himself that it would be no bad thing to know what became of the woman, tried to escape, bridle and all, from the stone. This he found, however, to be impossible, for as long as the bit was in his mouth, he was quite powerless to get away. So he managed, after a short struggle, to get the bridle off his head, and having so done, leapt into the precipice, down which he had seen Hildur disappear. After sinking for a long, long time, he caught a glimpse of Hildur beneath him, and at last they came to some beautiful green meadows.

From all this, the man guessed that Hildur was by no means a common mortal, as she had before made believe to be, and feared if he were to follow her along these green fields, and she turn round and catch sight of him, he might, not unlikely, pay for his curiosity with his life. So he took a magic stone which he always carried about him, the nature of which was to make him invisible when he held it in his palm, and placing it in the hollow of his hand, ran after her with all his strength.

When they had gone some way along the meadows, a splendid palace rose before them, with the way to which Hildur seemed perfectly well acquainted. At her approach a great crowd of people came forth from the doors, and saluted Hildur with respect and joy. Foremost of these walked a man of kingly and noble aspect, whose salutation seemed to be that of a lover or a husband: all the rest bowed to her as if she were their queen. This man was accompanied by two children, who ran up to Hildur, calling her mother, and embraced her. After the people had welcomed their queen, they all returned to the palace, where they dressed her in royal robes, and loaded her hands with costly rings and bracelets.

The herdsman followed the crowd, and posted himself where he would be least in the way of the company, but where he could catch sight easily of all that passed, and lose nothing. So gorgeous and dazzling were the hangings of the hall, and the silver and golden vessels on the table, that he thought he had never, in all his life before, seen the like; not to mention the wonderful dishes and wines which seemed plentiful there, and which, only by the look of them, filled his mouth with water, while he would much rather have filled it with something else.

After he had waited a little time, Hildur appeared in the hall, and all the assembled guests were begged to take their seats, while Hildur sat on her throne beside the king; after which all the people of the court ranged themselves on each side of the royal couple, and the feast commenced.

When it was concluded, the various guests amused themselves, some by dancing, some by singing, others by drinking and revel; but the king and queen talked together, and seemed to the herdsman to be very sad.

While they were thus conversing, three children, younger than those the man had seen before, ran in, and clung round the neck of their mother. Hildur received them with all a mother's love, and, as the youngest was restless, put it on the ground and gave it one of her rings to play with.

After the little one had played a while with the ring he lost it, and it rolled along the floor towards the herdsman, who, being invisible, picked it up without being perceived, and put it carefully into his pocket. Of course a search for it by the guests was in vain.

When the night was far advanced, Hildur made preparations for departure, at which all the people assembled showed great sorrow, and begged her to remain longer.

The herdsman had observed, that in one corner of the hall had sat an old and ugly woman, who had neither received the queen with joy nor pressed her to stay longer.

As soon as the king perceived that Hildur addressed herself to her journey, and that neither his entreaties nor those of the assembly could induce her to stay, he went up to the old woman, and said to her:

"Mother, rid us now of thy curse; cause no longer my queen to live apart and afar from me. Surely her short and rare visits are more pain to me than joy."

The old woman answered him with a wrathful face.

"Never will I depart from what I have said. My words shall hold true in all their force, and on no condition will I abolish my curse."

On this the king turned from her, and going up to his wife, entreated her in the fondest and most loving terms not to depart from him.

The queen answered, "The infernal power of thy mother's curse forces me to go, and perchance this may be the last time that I shall see thee. For lying, as I do, under this horrible ban, it is not possible that my constant murders can remain much longer secret, and then I must suffer the full penalty of crimes which I have committed against my will."

While she was thus speaking the herdsman sped from the palace and across the fields to the precipice, up which he mounted as rapidly as he had come down, thanks to the magic stone.

When he arrived at the rock he put the stone into his pocket, and the bridle over his head again, and awaited the coming of the elf-queen. He had not long to wait, for very soon afterwards Hildur came up through the abyss, and mounted on his back, and off they flew again to the farmhouse, where Hildur, taking the bridle from his head, placed him again in his bed, and retired to her own. The herdsman, who by this time was well tired out, now considered it safe to go to sleep, which he did, so soundly as not to wake till quite late on Christmas-morning.

Early that same day the farmer rose, agitated and filled with the fear that, instead of passing Christmas in joy, he should assuredly, as he so often had before, find his herdsman dead, and pass it in sorrow and mourning. So he and all the rest of the family went to the bedside of the herdsman.

When the farmer had looked at him and found him breathing, he praised God aloud for his mercy in preserving the man from death.

Not long afterwards the man himself awoke and got up.

Wondering at his strange preservation the farmer asked him how he had passed the night, and whether he had seen or heard anything.

The man replied, "No; but I have had a very curious dream."

"What was it?" asked the farmer.

Upon which the man related everything that had passed in the night, circumstance for circumstance, and word for word, as well as he could remember. When he had finished his story everyone was silent for wonder, except Hildur, who went up to him and said:

"I declare you to be a liar in all that you have said, unless you can prove it by sure evidence."

Not in the least abashed, the herdsman took from his pocket the ring which he had picked up on the floor of the hall in Elf-land, and showing it to her said:

"Though my dream needs no proof, yet here is one you will not doubtless deem other than a sure one; for is not this your gold ring, Queen Hildur?"

Hildur answered, "It is, no doubt, my ring. Happy man! may you prosper in all you undertake, for you have released me from the awful yoke which my mother-in-law laid, in her wrath, upon me, and from the curse of a yearly murder."

And then Hildur told them the story of her life as follows:—

"I was born of an obscure family among the elves. Our king fell in love with me and married me, in spite of the strong disapproval of his mother. She swore eternal hatred to me in her anger against her son, and said to him, 'Short shall be your joy with this fair wife of yours, for you shall see her but once a year, and that only at the expense of a murder. This is my curse upon her, and it shall be carried out to the letter. She shall go and serve in the upper world, this queen, and every Christmas-eve shall ride a man, one of her fellow-servants, with this magic bridle, to the confines of Elf-land, where she shall pass a few hours with you, and then ride him back again till his very heart breaks with toil, and his very life leaves him. Let her thus enjoy her queenship.'

"And this horrible fate was to cling to me until I should either have these murders brought home to me, and be condemned to death, or should meet with a gallant man, like this herdsman, who should have nerve and courage to follow me down into Elf-land, and be able to prove afterwards that he had been there with me, and seen the customs of my people. And now I must confess that all the former herdsmen were slain by me, but no penalty shall touch me for their murders, as I committed them against my will. And as for you, O courageous man, who have dared, the first of human beings, to explore the realms of Elf-land, and have freed me from the yoke of this awful curse, I will reward you in times to come, but not now.

"A deep longing for my home and my loved ones impels me hence. Farewell!"

With these words Hildur vanished from the sight of the astonished people, and was never seen again.

But our friend the herdsman, leaving the service of the farmer, built a farm for himself, and prospered, and became one of the chief men in the country, and always ascribed, with grateful thanks, his prosperity to Hildur, Queen of the Elves.

THE WIDOW'S SON

Norway

There was once a poor, very poor widow, who had an only son. She pulled through with the boy till he was confirmed; but then she told him that she could not feed him any longer; he would have to go out and earn his own bread.

The lad wandered out into the world, and when he had walked a day or so he met a stranger.—"Where are you going to?" asked the man.—"I'm going out into the world to try and get some work," said the lad.—"Will you come into my service?" asked the man.—"Well, why not! just as well with you as with anybody else," answered the lad.—"You will find it a very good place," said the man; "you are only going to keep me company and do nothing else besides."

So the lad went with him home, and he got plenty of food and drink, and had little or nothing to do; but on the other hand he never saw a living soul come near the man.

So one day the man said to him: "I'm going away for eight days, and during that time you will be here all alone, but you must not go into any of these four rooms here. If you do I will take your life when I come back."— No, said the lad, he should not go into any of the rooms.

But when the man had been away three or four days the lad could not help going into one of the rooms. He looked round, but saw nothing but a shelf over the door, on which lay a brier twig. Well, this is surely something to forbid my seeing, thought the boy.

When the eight days were gone the man returned.—"You haven't been into any of the rooms, I suppose?" said he.—"No, not at all," said the lad.—"Well, we shall soon see," said the man, and with that he went into the room where the lad had been. "But I find you have been there after all," said the man, "and now you shall lose your life."

The lad cried and begged for himself till he got off with his life; but he got a good thrashing. When that was over they were as good friends as ever.

Some time afterwards the man went away again; he was going to stay away for a fortnight this time, but first he told the lad that he must not put a foot in any of the rooms where he had not already been; he might, however, go into that room where he had been.

Well, it happened just as the last time, only that the lad waited eight days before he went into the second room. In this room he saw nothing but a shelf over the door, and a piece of rock and a water-jug on it. Well, that's something to be so afraid of, thought the lad again.

When the man came back he asked the lad if he had been into any of the rooms.—No, not likely, the lad hadn't been there!—"We shall soon see," said the man, but when he saw that the lad had been into one of the rooms after all, he said: "I shall spare you no longer now; you will lose your life this time!"

But the lad cried and begged for himself again, and he got off with a good thrashing again, but this time he got as much as he could possibly stand. When he had got over the effects of the thrashing he led the same comfortable life as before, and he and the man were the best of friends again.

Some time after the man had to go on a journey again, and this time he should be away for three weeks, and so he said to the lad that if he went into the third room during his absence, he would not have the slightest chance of escaping with his life.

When fourteen days had gone the lad could not help himself; but stole into the third room; he saw nothing in there except a trap-door in the floor. When he lifted it up and looked down into the room below he saw a big copper kettle which stood there and boiled and bubbled; but he saw no fire under it.

It would be great fun to feel if it is hot, thought the boy, and put his finger into the kettle, but when he pulled it out again it was gilded all over. The boy scraped and washed it, but the gilding would not come off, so he tied a rag round it, and when the man came home and asked what was the matter with his finger the lad said that he had cut himself very badly. But the man tore off the rag, and then he saw easily enough what really ailed the finger.

He was at first going to kill the lad; but as he began crying and praying for himself again, he gave him such a sound thrashing instead that he had to keep his bed for three days, and then the man took a jar down from the wall, and rubbed the lad with some of its contents and he was as well as ever again.

Before long the man went away again, and was not coming back for a month. But he told the lad that if he went into the fourth room he must not have any hope of escaping with his life that time.

For two or three weeks the lad managed to resist the temptation, but then he couldn't help himself any longer,—he must and would go into that room, and so he did. There stood a big black horse in a box by himself, and with a manger of glowing cinders at his head, and a truss of hay at his tail. The lad thought this was altogether wrong; he changed them about and put the truss of hay at the horse's head.

So the horse said: "Since you have such a good heart that you let me have something to eat, I will save you from the troll, for that's what the man is that you are with. But now you must go up into the room just above here and take a suit of armour out of those hanging there, and mind you do not take any of the bright ones, but the most rusty you see. Take that one! And sword and saddle you must look out for yourself in the same way."

The lad did as he was told, but it was very heavy work to carry it all at once. When he came back the horse told him to take all his clothes off and jump into the kettle which stood and boiled in the room below, and to have a good dip there.

"I shall be an awful sight then," thought the lad, but he did as the horse had told him. When he had finished his bath he became handsome and smart, and as red and white as blood and milk, and much stronger than before.

"Do you feel any different?" asked the horse.—"Yes," said the lad.—"Try if you can lift me," said the horse.—Oh, yes, he could do that; and the sword, why, he swung it about his head as if it were nothing at all. "Now, put the saddle on me," said the horse, "and put the suit of armour on you, and then don't forget the brier-twig, the piece of rock, the water-jug, and the jar of ointment, and then we'll be off."

The lad had no sooner got on the horse than off they went at such a rate that he couldn't tell how fast they got on. When he had been riding for some time the horse said to him: "I think I hear a rumbling of something! Just look round; can you see anything?"—"Yes, there are a great, great many coming after us; at least a score," said the lad.—"Well, that's the troll," said the horse; "he is coming after us with his imps."

They rode on for a while, until they who were coming after them were close upon them. "Now throw your brier-twig over your shoulder," said the horse, "but throw it a good distance behind me!" The lad did so, and suddenly a big, close brier-wood grew up behind them. So the lad rode a long, long way, while the troll had to go home and fetch something to hew his way through the wood.

But in a while the horse said again: "Look behind! Can you see anything now?"—"Yes, a great many," said the lad; "as many as would fill a church."—"Ah ha! that's the troll,—he has taken more with him this time. Throw the piece of rock you have, but throw it far behind me!"

As soon as the lad had done what the horse had said, a great steep mountain rose behind him, and so the troll had to go home and fetch something to mine his way through the mountain, and while the troll was doing this the lad rode again some distance on his way. But before long the horse asked him to look behind him again, and then the lad saw a crowd like a big army in bright armour, which glistened in the sun. "Ah ha!" said the horse, "that's the troll,—now he has got all his imps with him. Take the water-jug and throw all the water out behind you, but mind you do not spill any of it on me!"

The lad did as he was told, but for all the care he took, he happened to spill a drop on the horse's flank. Well, the water he threw behind him became a great lake, but on account of the drop he spilled on the horse he found himself far out in the water, but the horse swam safely to land with him. When the trolls came to the lake they laid down to drink it dry, but they drank till they burst. "Now we have got rid of them," said the horse.

So when they had travelled a long, long time, they came to a green plain in a wood. "Now you must take off your whole suit of armour and only put your own ragged clothes on," said the horse, "and then take the saddle off me and let me go; but hang all the things inside this big hollow lime-tree here. You must then make yourself a wig of pine-moss and go up to the king's palace, which is close by; there you must ask for service. Whenever you want me, only come and shake the bridle, and I'll come to you."

Yes, the lad did as the horse had told him, and when he put the wig of moss on his head he became so ugly, and pale, and miserable looking that no one would know him again. He then went to the palace and asked first, if he could get some work in the kitchen and carry water and wood for the cook; but the cook asked: "Why do you wear that ugly wig? Take it off you! I won't have such a fright in here."—"I can't do that," answered the lad, "I am not all right in my head."— "Do you think I will have you here near the food, if that's the case?" said the cook; "go down to the coachman; you are better suited for cleaning out the stable."

But when the coachman asked him to take off his wig and got the same answer he would not have him either. "You had better go to the gardener," he said; "you are more fit for digging in the garden." Yes, the gardener would take him, and gave him leave to stay with him, but none of the other servants would sleep with him, so he had to sleep by himself under the steps of the summer-house. It stood on posts, and a high staircase led up to it; under this he put some moss for a bed, and there he lay as well as he could.

When he had been some time at the palace, it happened one morning, just as the sun was rising, that the lad had taken off his wig of moss and was washing himself; he then looked so handsome that it was a pleasure to look at him.

The princess saw the lad from her window, and she thought that she never had seen any one so handsome. She asked the gardener why the lad slept out there under the steps. "Oh, none of his fellow-servants will sleep with him," said the gardener. "Let him come up and lie outside the door of my chamber," said the princess, "and then I suppose they will not think themselves too good to sleep in the same room as he."

The gardener told the lad of it. "Do you think I'll do that?" said the lad; "they would say that I was running after the princess."—"Yes, you are very likely to be suspected of that," said the gardener, "you are so good-looking!"—"Well, if she orders it so, I suppose I must go," said the lad.

When he was going up stairs in the evening he tramped and stamped so terribly that they had to tell him to walk more softly, that the king should not get to know it. So he lay down by the door and began to snore.

The princess then said to her maid: "Just go quietly to him and pull off his wig." The maid was just going to snatch it off his head, when he took hold of it with both his hands and said that she should not have it; and with that he lay down again and began snoring. The princess gave the maid a sign again, and that time she snatched the wig off him, and there lay the lad so lovely and red and white, just as the princess had seen him in the morning sun. After that the lad slept every night outside the princess's chamber.

But before long the king got to hear that the gardener's boy lay outside the princess's chamber every night, and he was so enraged at this that he almost took the lad's life. He did not do this, however, but threw him into the prison tower. He shut up his daughter in her chamber, and told her she should not have leave to go out day or night. She cried and prayed for herself and the lad, but all to no purpose. The king only got more vexed at it.

In a while a war broke out in the land, and the king had to take up arms against another king, who wanted to take the kingdom from him. When the lad heard this he asked the keeper to go to the king and ask for a suit of armour and a sword and permission to go to the war. All laughed when the keeper delivered his message, and asked the king to give him some old rusty suit, that they might have the fun of seeing this poor wretch going to fight in the war. So the lad got permission and an old, wretched horse in the bargain, who jogged along on three legs and dragged the fourth after him.

So they all set out to meet the enemy; but they had not got far from the palace before the lad got stuck in a bog with his nag. There he sat and kicked away and cried: "Gee up, gee up!" to his nag. All amused themselves at this sight, and laughed and made game of the lad as they rode past.

But no sooner were they out of sight than the lad ran to the lime-tree, put on his suit of armour, and shook the bridle. The horse appeared at once, and said: "You do your best, and I will do mine!" When the lad came up the battle had already begun, and the king was in a bad plight; but the lad rushed into the thick of the fight and put the enemy to flight. The king and his people wondered much who it could be who had come to help them; but no one came so near him as to be able to talk to him, and when the battle was over he was gone. When they rode home, they found the lad still stuck in the bog, kicking away at his three-legged nag, and they began laughing again. "Just look! there sits that fool still!" they said.

The next day when they set out again, the lad was still sitting there; they laughed again and made game of him, but no sooner had they ridden past him, before the lad ran to the lime-tree, and all happened just as on the first day. Every one wondered who this strange warrior could be that had helped the king. No one, of course, guessed it could be the lad!

When they were on their way home at night and saw the lad still sitting there on his horse, they jeered at him again, and one of them shot an arrow at him and hit him in the leg. He began to cry and wail so pitiably, that the king threw his pocket-handkerchief to him to tie round the wound. The third morning when they set out, they found the lad still on his nag in the bog. "Gee up, gee up!" he was shouting to his horse. "I am afraid he will be sitting there till he starves to death," said one of the king's soldiers, as they rode past him, and laughed at him till they were nearly falling off their horses. But when they were gone, he ran again to the lime-tree, and came up to the battle in the very nick of time. That day he killed the king of the enemy, and so the war was all over.

When the battle was over, the king happened to discover his handkerchief, which the strange warrior had tied round his leg, and he had no difficulty then in guessing who he was. They received him with great joy, and brought him with them to the palace, and the princess, who saw him from her window, became so glad, that no one could believe it, and she exclaimed joyfully: "There comes my love."

He then took the pot of ointment and rubbed himself on the leg, and afterwards he rubbed all the wounded, so that all were well there and then.

So he married the princess, but on the very day when the wedding took place, he went down into the stable to his horse, who was standing there quite sullen and dejected; his ears hung down, and he would not eat anything. When the young king—for he was now made king, and had got half the kingdom—spoke to him and asked what was the matter with him, the horse said: "I have now helped you through, and I do not care to live any longer. You must take the sword and cut my head off."

"No, I will do nothing of the sort," said the young king; "but you shall have everything you want and do no more work."—"Well, if you don't do as I tell you," said the horse, "you had better look out for your life, which is in my hands entirely." So the king had to do what was asked of him; but when he lifted the sword and was about to strike, he felt so grieved that he had to turn his face away, because he would not see the blow; but no sooner had he cut the head off, than the loveliest prince stood on the spot where the horse had stood.

"Where in all the world did you come from?" asked the king.

"It was I who was the horse," answered the prince. "At one time I was king in the land where the king came from that you killed in the battle yesterday. It was he who turned me into a horse and sold me to the troll. But now that he is killed, I shall get my kingdom back again, and you and I will be neighbouring kings; but we will never make war on one another."

And no more they did; they were friends as long as they lived, and they used to go and visit each other very often.

TOLLER'S NEIGHBOURS

Denmark

Once upon a time a young man and a young girl were in service together at a mansion down near Klode Mill, in the district of Lysgaard. They became attached to each other, and as they both were honest and faithful servants, their master and mistress had a great regard for them, and gave them a wedding dinner the day they were married. Their master gave them also a little cottage with a little field, and there they went to live.

This cottage lay in the middle of a wild heath, and the surrounding country was in bad repute; for in the neighbourhood were a number of old grave-mounds, which it was said were inhabited by the Mount-folk; though Toller, so the peasant was called, cared little for that. "When one only trusts in God," thought Toller, "and does what is just and right to all men, one need not be afraid of anything." They had now taken possession of their cottage and moved in all their little property. When the man and his wife, late one evening, were sitting talking together as to how they could best manage to get on in the world, they heard a knock at the door, and on Toller opening it, in walked a little little man, and wished them "Good evening." He had a red cap on his head, a long beard and long hair, a large hump on his back, and a leathern apron before him, in which was stuck a hammer. They immediately knew him to be a Troll; notwithstanding he looked so good-natured and friendly, that they were not at all afraid of him.

"Now hear, Toller," said the little stranger, "I see well enough that you know who I am, and matters stand thus. I am a poor little hill-man, to whom people have left no other habitation on earth than the graves of fallen warriors, or mounds, where the rays of the sun never can shine down upon us. We have heard that you are come to live here, and our king is fearful that you will do us harm, and even destroy us. He has, therefore, sent me up to you this evening, that I should beg of you, as amicably as I could, to allow us to hold our dwellings in peace. You shall never be annoyed by us, or disturbed by us in your pursuits."

"Be quite at your ease, good man," said Toller, "I have never injured any of God's creatures willingly, and the world is large enough for us all, I believe; and I think we can manage to agree, without the one having any need to do mischief to the other."

"Well, thank God!" exclaimed the little man, beginning in his joy to dance about the room, "that is excellent, and we will in return do you all the good in our power, and that you will soon discover; but now I must depart."

"Will you not first take a spoonful of supper with us?" asked the wife, setting a dish of porridge down on the stool near the window; for the Man of the Mount was so little that he could not reach up to the table. "No, I thank you," said the mannikin, "our king is impatient for my return and it would be a pity to let him wait for the good news I have to tell him." Hereupon the little man bade them farewell and went his way.

From that day forwards, Toller lived in peace and concord with the little people of the Mount. They could see them go in and out of their mounds in daylight, and no one ever did anything to vex them. At length they became so familiar, that they went in and out of Toller's house, just as if it had been their own. Sometimes it happened that they would borrow a pot or a copper-kettle from the kitchen, but always brought it back again, and set it carefully on the same spot from which they had taken it. They also did all the service they could in return. When the spring came, they would come out of their mounds in the night, gathering all the stones off the arable land, and lay them in a heap along the furrows. At harvest time they would pick up all the ears of corn, that nothing might be lost to Toller. All this was observed by the farmer, who, when in bed, or when he read his evening prayer, often thanked the Almighty for having given him the Mount-folk for neighbours. At Easter and Whitsuntide, or in the Christmas holidays, he always set a dish of nice milk-porridge for them, as good as it could be made, out on the mound.

Once, after having given birth to a daughter, his wife was so ill that Toller thought she was near her end. He consulted all the cunning people in the district, but no one knew what to prescribe for her recovery. He sat up every night and watched over the sufferer, that he might be at hand to administer to her wants. Once he fell asleep, and on opening his eyes again towards morning, he saw the room full of the Mount-folk: one sat and rocked the baby, another was busy in cleaning the room, a third stood by the pillow of the sick woman and made a drink of some herbs, which he gave his wife. As soon as they observed that Toller was awake they all ran out of the room; but from that night the poor woman began to mend, and before a fortnight was past she was able to leave her bed and go about her household work, well and cheerful as before.

Another time, Toller was in trouble for want of money to get his horses shod before he went to the town. He talked the matter over with his wife, and they knew not well what course to adopt. But when they were in bed his wife said: "Art thou asleep, Toller?" "No," he answered, "what is it?" "I think," said she, "there is something the matter with the horses in the stable, they are making such a disturbance." Toller rose, lighted his lantern, and went to the stable, and, on opening the door, found it full of the little Mount-folk. They had made the horses lie down, because the mannikins could not reach up to them. Some were employed in taking off the old shoes, some were filing the heads of the nails, while others were tacking on the new shoes; and the next morning, when Toller took his horses to water, he found them shod so beautifully that the best of smiths could not have shod them better. In this manner the Mount-folk and Toller rendered all the good services they could to each other, and many years passed pleasantly. Toller began to grow an old man, his daughter was grown up, and his circumstances were better every year. Instead of the little cottage in which he began the world, he now owned a large and handsome house, and the naked wild heath was converted into fruitful arable land.

One evening just before bed-time, some one knocked at the door, and the Man of the Mount walked in. Toller and his wife looked at him with surprise; for the mannikin was not in his usual dress. He wore on his head a shaggy cap, a woollen kerchief round his throat, and a great sheep-skin cloak covered his body. In his hand he had a stick, and his countenance was very sorrowful. He brought a greeting to Toller from the king, who requested that he, his wife, and little Inger would come over to them in the Mount that evening, for the king had a matter of importance, about which he wished to talk with him. The tears ran down the little man's cheeks while he said this, and when Toller tried to comfort him, and inquired into the source of his trouble, the Man of the Mount only wept the more, but would not impart the cause of his grief.

Toller, his wife and daughter, then went over to the Mount. On descending into the cave, they found it decorated with bunches of sweet willow, crowfoots, and other flowers, that were to be found on the heath. A large table was spread from one end of the cave to the other. When the peasant and his family entered, they were placed at the head of the table by the side of the king. The little folk also took their places, and began to eat, but they were far from being as cheerful as usual; they sat and sighed and hung down their heads; and it was easy to see that something had gone amiss with them. When the repast was finished, the king said to Toller: "I invited you to come over to us because we all wished to thank you for having been so kind and friendly to us, during the whole time we have been neighbours. But now there are so many churches built in the land, and all of them have such great bells, which ring so loud morning and evening, that we can bear it no longer; we are, therefore, going to leave Jutland and pass over to Norway, as the greater number of our people have done long ago. We now wish you farewell, Toller, as we must part."

When the king had said this, all the Mount-folk came and took Toller by the hand, and bade him farewell, and the same to his wife. When they came to Inger, they said: "To you, dear Inger, we will give a remembrance of us, that you may think of the little Mount-people when they are far away." And as they said this, each took up a stone from the ground and threw it into Inger's apron. They left the Mount one by one, with the king leading the way.

Toller and his family remained standing on the Mount as long as they could discern them. They saw the little Trolls wandering over the heath, each with a wallet on his back and a stick in his hand. When they had gone a good part of the way, to where the road leads down to the sea, they all turned round once more, and waved their hands, to say farewell. Then they disappeared, and Toller saw them no more. Sorrowfully he returned to his home.

The next morning Inger saw that all the small stones the Mount-folk had thrown into her apron shone and sparkled, and were real precious stones. Some were blue, others brown, white, and black, and it was the Trolls who had imparted the colour of their eyes to the stones, that Inger might remember them when they were gone; and all the precious stones which we now see, shine and sparkle only because the Mount-folk have given them the colour of their eyes, and it was some of these beautiful precious stones which they once gave to Inger.

WIT

MIGHTY MIKKO:
THE STORY of a
POOR WOODSMAN and a
GRATEFUL FOX

Finland

There was once an old woodsman and his wife who had an only son named Mikko. As the mother lay dying the young man wept bitterly.

"When you are gone, my dear mother," he said, "there will be no one left to think of me."

The poor woman comforted him as best she could and said to him:

"You will still have your father."

Shortly after the woman's death, the old man, too, was taken ill.

"Now, indeed, I shall be left desolate and alone," Mikko thought, as he sat beside his father's bedside and saw him grow weaker and weaker.

"My boy," the old man said just before he died, "I have nothing to leave you but the three snares with which these many years I have caught wild animals. Those snares now belong to you. When I am dead, go into the woods and if you find a wild creature caught in any of them, free it gently and bring it home alive."

After his father's death, Mikko remembered the snares and went out to the woods to see them. The first was empty and also the second, but in the third he found a little red Fox. He carefully lifted the spring that had shut down on one of the Fox's feet and then carried the little creature home in his arms. He shared his supper with it and when he lay down to sleep the Fox curled up at his feet. They lived together some time until they became close friends.

"Mikko," said the Fox one day, "why are you so sad?"

"Because I'm lonely."

"Pooh!" said the Fox. "That's no way for a young man to talk! You ought to get married! Then you wouldn't feel lonely!"

"Married!" Mikko repeated. "How can I get married? I can't marry a poor girl because I'm too poor myself and a rich girl wouldn't marry me."

"Nonsense!" said the Fox. "You're a fine well set up young man and you're kind and gentle. What more could a princess ask?"

Mikko laughed to think of a princess wanting him for a husband.

"I mean what I say!" the Fox insisted. "Take our own Princess now. What would you think of marrying her?"

Mikko laughed louder than before.

"I have heard," he said, "that she is the most beautiful princess in the world! Any man would be happy to marry her!"

"Very well," the Fox said, "if you feel that way about her then I'll arrange the wedding for you."

With that the little Fox actually did trot off to the royal castle and gain audience with the King.

"My master sends you greetings," the Fox said, "and he begs you to loan him your bushel measure."

"My bushel measure!" the King repeated in surprise. "Who is your master and why does he want my bushel measure?"

"Ssh!" the Fox whispered as though he didn't want the courtiers to hear what he was saying. Then slipping up quite close to the King he murmured in his ear:

"Surely you have heard of Mikko, haven't you?—Mighty Mikko as he's called."

The King had never heard of any Mikko who was known as Mighty Mikko but, thinking that perhaps he should have heard of him, he shook his head and murmured:

"H'm! Mikko! Mighty Mikko! Oh, to be sure! Yes, yes, of course!"

"My master is about to start off on a journey and he needs a bushel measure for a very particular reason."

"I understand! I understand!" the King said, although he didn't understand at all, and he gave orders that the bushel measure which they used in the storeroom of the castle be brought in and given to the Fox.

The Fox carried off the measure and hid it in the woods. Then he scurried about to all sorts of little out of the way nooks and crannies where people had hidden their savings and he dug up a gold piece here and a silver piece there until he had a handful. Then he went back to the woods and stuck the various coins in the cracks of the measure. The next day he returned to the King.

"My master, Mighty Mikko," he said, "sends you thanks, O King, for the use of your bushel measure."

The King held out his hand and when the Fox gave him the measure he peeped inside to see if by chance it contained any trace of what had recently been measured. His eye of course at once caught the glint of the gold and silver coins lodged in the cracks.

"Ah!" he said, thinking Mikko must be a very mighty lord indeed to be so careless of his wealth; "I should like to meet your master. Won't you and he come and visit me?"

This was what the Fox wanted the King to say but he pretended to hesitate.

"I thank your Majesty for the kind invitation," he said, "but I fear my master can't accept it just now. He wants to get married soon and we are about to start off on a long journey to inspect a number of foreign princesses."

This made the King all the more anxious to have Mikko visit him at once for he thought that if Mikko should see his daughter before he saw those foreign princesses he might fall in love with her and marry her. So he said to the Fox:

"My dear fellow, you must prevail on your master to make me a visit before he starts out on his travels! You will, won't you?"

The Fox looked this way and that as if he were too embarrassed to speak.

"Your Majesty," he said at last, "I pray you pardon my frankness. The truth is you are not rich enough to entertain my master and your castle isn't big enough to house the immense retinue that always attends him."

The King, who by this time was frantic to see Mikko, lost his head completely.

"My dear Fox," he said, "I'll give you anything in the world if you prevail upon your master to visit me at once! Couldn't you suggest to him to travel with a modest retinue this time?"

The Fox shook his head.

"No. His rule is either to travel with a great retinue or to go on foot disguised as a poor woodsman attended only by me."

"Couldn't you prevail on him to come to me disguised as a poor woodsman?" the

King begged. "Once he was here, I could place gorgeous clothes at his disposal."

But still the Fox shook his head.

"I fear Your Majesty's wardrobe doesn't contain the kind of clothes my master is accustomed to."

"I assure you I've got some very good clothes," the King said. "Come along this minute and we'll go through them and I'm sure you'll find some that your master would wear."

So they went to a room which was like a big wardrobe with hundreds and hundreds of hooks upon which were hung hundreds of coats and breeches and embroidered shirts. The King ordered his attendants to bring the costumes down one by one and place them before the Fox.

They began with the plainer clothes.

"Good enough for most people," the Fox said, "but not for my master."

Then they took down garments of a finer grade.

"I'm afraid you're going to all this trouble for nothing," the Fox said. "Frankly now, don't you realize that my master couldn't possibly put on any of these things!"

The King, who had hoped to keep for his own use his most gorgeous clothes of all, now ordered these to be shown.

The Fox looked at them sideways, sniffed them critically, and at last said:

"Well, perhaps my master would consent to wear these for a few days. They are not what he is accustomed to wear but I will say this for him: he is not proud."

The King was overjoyed.

"Very well, my dear Fox, I'll have the guest chambers put in readiness for your master's visit and I'll have all these, my finest clothes, laid out for him. You won't disappoint me, will you?"

"I'll do my best," the Fox promised.

With that he bade the King a civil good day and ran home to Mikko.

The next day as the Princess was peeping out of an upper window of the castle, she saw a young woodsman approaching accompanied by a Fox. He was a fine stalwart youth and the Princess, who knew from the presence of the Fox that he must be Mikko, gave a long sigh and confided to her serving maid:

"I think I could fall in love with that young man if he really were only a woodsman!"

Later when she saw him arrayed in her father's finest clothes—which looked so well on Mikko that no one even recognized them as the King's—she lost her heart completely and when Mikko was presented to her she blushed and trembled just as any ordinary girl might before a handsome young man.

All the Court was equally delighted with Mikko. The ladies went into ecstasies over his modest manners, his fine figure, and the gorgeousness of his clothes, and the old graybeard Councilors, nodding their heads in approval, said to each other:

"Nothing of the coxcomb about this young fellow! In spite of his great wealth see how politely he listens to us when we talk!"

The next day the Fox went privately to the King, and said:

"My master is a man of few words and quick judgment. He bids me tell you that your daughter, the Princess, pleases him mightily and that, with your approval, he will make his addresses to her at once."

The King was greatly agitated and began:

"My dear Fox—"

But the Fox interrupted him to say:

"Think the matter over carefully and give me your decision to-morrow."

So the King consulted with the Princess and with his Councilors and in a short time the marriage was arranged and the wedding ceremony actually performed!

"Didn't I tell you?" the Fox said, when he and Mikko were alone after the wedding.

"Yes," Mikko acknowledged, "you did promise that I should marry the Princess. But, tell me, now that I am married what am I to do? I can't live on here forever with my wife."

"Put your mind at rest," the Fox said. "I've thought of everything. Just do as I tell you and you'll have nothing to regret. To-night say to the King: 'It is now only fitting that you should visit me and see for yourself the sort of castle over which your daughter is hereafter to be mistress!'"

When Mikko said this to the King, the King was overjoyed for now that the marriage had actually taken place he was wondering whether he hadn't perhaps been a little hasty. Mikko's words reassured him and he eagerly accepted the invitation.

On the morrow the Fox said to Mikko:

"Now I'll run on ahead and get things ready for you."

"But where are you going?" Mikko said, frightened at the thought of being deserted by his little friend.

The Fox drew Mikko aside and whispered softly:

"A few days' march from here there is a very gorgeous castle belonging to a wicked old dragon who is known as the Worm. I think the Worm's castle would just about suit you."

"I'm sure it would," Mikko agreed. "But how are we to get it away from the Worm?"

"Trust me," the Fox said. "All you need do is this: lead the King and his courtiers along the main highway until by noon to-morrow you reach a crossroads. Turn there to the left and go straight on until you see the tower of the Worm's castle. If you meet any men by the wayside, shepherds or the like, ask them whose men they are and show no surprise at their answer. So now, dear master, farewell until we meet again at your beautiful castle."

The little Fox trotted off at a smart pace and Mikko and the Princess and the King attended by the whole Court followed in more leisurely fashion.

The little Fox, when he had left the main highway at the crossroads, soon met ten woodsmen with axes over their shoulders. They were all dressed in blue smocks of the same cut.

"Good day," the Fox said politely. "Whose men are you?"

"Our master is known as the Worm," the woodsmen told him.

"My poor, poor lads!" the Fox said, shaking his head sadly.

"What's the matter?" the woodsmen asked.

For a few moments the Fox pretended to be too overcome with emotion to speak. Then he said:

"My poor lads, don't you know that the King is coming with a great force to destroy the Worm and all his people?"

The woodsmen were simple fellows and this news threw them into great consternation.

"Is there no way for us to escape?" they asked.

The Fox put his paw to his head and thought.

"Well," he said at last, "there is one way you might escape and that is by telling every one who asks you that you are the Mighty Mikko's men. But if you value your lives never again say that your master is the Worm."

"We are Mighty Mikko's men!" the woodsmen at once began repeating over and over. "We are Mighty Mikko's men!"

A little farther on the road the Fox met twenty grooms, dressed in the same blue smocks, who were tending a hundred beautiful horses. The Fox talked to the twenty grooms as he had talked to the woodsmen and before he left them they, too, were shouting:

"We are Mighty Mikko's men!"

Next the Fox came to a huge flock of a thousand sheep tended by thirty shepherds all dressed in the Worm's blue smocks. He stopped and talked to them until he had them roaring out:

"We are Mighty Mikko's men!"

Then the Fox trotted on until he reached the castle of the Worm. He found the Worm himself inside lolling lazily about. He was a huge dragon and had been a great warrior in his day. In fact his castle and his lands and his servants and his possessions had all been won in battle. But now for many years no one had cared to fight him and he had grown fat and lazy.

"Good day," the Fox said, pretending to be very breathless and frightened. "You're the Worm, aren't you?"

"Yes," the dragon said, boastfully, "I am the great Worm!"

The Fox pretended to grow more agitated.

"My poor fellow, I am sorry for you! But of course none of us can expect to live forever. Well, I must hurry along. I thought I would just stop and say good-by."

Made uneasy by the Fox's words, the Worm cried out:

"Wait just a minute! What's the matter?"

The Fox was already at the door but at the Worm's entreaty he paused and said over his shoulder:

"Why, my poor fellow, you surely know, don't you? that the King with a great force is coming to destroy you and all your people!"

"What!" the Worm gasped, turning a sickly green with fright. He knew he was fat and helpless and could never again fight as in the years gone by.

"Don't go just yet!" he begged the Fox. "When is the King coming?"

"He's on the highway now! That's why I must be going! Good-by!"

"My dear Fox, stay just a moment and I'll reward you richly! Help me to hide so that the King won't find me! What about the shed where the linen is stored? I could crawl under the linen and then if you locked the door from the outside the King could never find me."

"Very well," the Fox agreed, "but we must hurry!"

So they ran outside to the shed where the linen was kept and the Worm hid himself under the linen. The Fox locked the door, then set fire to the shed, and soon there was nothing left of that wicked old dragon, the Worm, but a handful of ashes.

The Fox now called together the dragon's household and talked them over to Mikko as he had the woodsmen and the grooms and the shepherds.

Meanwhile the King and his party were slowly covering the ground over which the Fox had sped so quickly. When they came to the ten woodsmen in blue smocks, the King said:

"I wonder whose woodsmen those are."

One of his attendants asked the woodsmen and the ten of them shouted out at the top of their voices:

"We are Mighty Mikko's men!"

Mikko said nothing and the King and all the Court were impressed anew with his modesty.

A little farther on they met the twenty grooms with their hundred prancing horses. When the grooms were questioned, they answered with a shout:

"We are Mighty Mikko's men!"

"The Fox certainly spoke the truth," the King thought to himself, "when he told me of Mikko's riches!"

A little later the thirty shepherds when they were questioned made answer in a chorus that was deafening to hear:

"We are Mighty Mikko's men!"

The sight of the thousand sheep that belonged to his son-in-law made the King feel poor and humble in comparison and the courtiers whispered among themselves:

"For all his simple manner, Mighty Mikko must be a richer, more powerful lord than the King himself! In fact it is only a very great lord in____ who could be so simple!"

At last they reached the castle which from the blue smo____ soldiers that guarded the gateway they knew to be Mikko's. The Fox came ou____ welcome the King's party and behind him in two rows all the household serva____ These, at a signal from the Fox, cried out in one voice:

"We are Mighty Mikko's men!"

Then Mikko in the same simple manner that he would have used ____ his father's mean little hut in the woods bade the King and his followers welc____ and they all entered the castle where they found a great feast already prepar____ and waiting.

The King stayed on for several days and the more he saw o____ ko the better pleased he was that he had him for a son-in-law.

When he was leaving he said to Mikko:

"Your castle is so much grander than mine that I hesi____ ever asking you back for a visit."

But Mikko reassured the King by saying earnestl____

"My dear father-in-law, when first I entered ____ astle I thought it was the most beautiful castle in the world!"

The King was flattered and the courtiers ____ red among themselves:

"How affable of him to say that when ____ ws very well how much grander his own castle is!"

When the King and his follow____ safely gone, the little red Fox came to Mikko and said:

"Now, my master, you h____ o reason to feel sad and lonely. You are lord of the most beautiful castle i____ e world and you have for wife a sweet and lovely Princess. You have no l____ er any need of me, so I am going to bid you farewell."

Mikko thanked th____ ttle Fox for all he had done and the little Fox trotted off to the woods.

So you see that M____ o's poor old father, although he had no wealth to leave his son, was really the ____ e of all Mikko's good fortune, for it was he who told Mikko in the first place t____ rry home alive anything he might find caught in the snares.

OLD NICK and the GIRL

Sweden

There was once a girl who was so mad about dancing that she nearly went out of her mind whenever she heard a fiddle strike up.

She was a very clever dancer, and a smarter girl to whirl round in a dance or kick her heels was not easily to be found, although she only had shoes made of birch-bark, and knitted leggings on her feet. She swept past at such a rate that the air whistled round her like a humming top. She might have whirled round still more quickly and lightly, of course, if she had had leather shoes. But how was she to get them, when she had no money to pay for them? For she was very poor, this girl, and could ill afford them.

So one day, when the fair was being held at Amberg Heath, whom should she meet but Old Nick![1] He was going to see the fun of the fair, as you may guess, for all sorts of tramps and vagabonds and watch-dealers and rogues go there; and where such gentry are to be found, others of the same feather are sure to flock together.

"What are you thinking about?" asked Old Nick, who knew well enough how matters stood.

"I am wondering how I shall be able to get a pair of leather shoes to dance in," said the girl; "for I haven't any money to pay for them," she said.

"Is that all? We'll soon get over that," said Old Nick, and produced a pair of leather shoes, which he showed her. "Do you like these?" he asked.

---

1.   Another name for the Devil.

The girl stood staring at the shoes. She could never have believed that there were such fine, splendid shoes, for they were not common ones sewn with pitched thread, but real German shoes with welted soles, and looked as French as one could wish.

"Is there a spring in them as well?" she asked.

"Yes, that you may be sure of," said Old Nick. "Do you want them?"

Yes, that she did; there could be no doubt about that, and so they began bargaining and higgling about the payment, till at last they came to terms. She was to have the shoes for a whole year for nothing, if only she would dance in his interest, and afterwards she should belong to him.

She did not exactly make a good bargain, but Old Nick is not a person one can bargain with. But there was to be such a spring in them that no human being would be able to swing round quicker in a dance or kick higher than she did; and if they did not satisfy her, he would take them back for nothing, and she should be free.

With this they parted.

And now the girl seemed to wake up thoroughly. She thought of nothing else but going to dances, wherever they might be, night after night. Well, she danced and danced, and before she knew it the year came to an end, and Old Nick came and asked for his due.

"They were a rubbishy pair of shoes you gave me," said the girl; "there was no spring at all in them," she said.

"Wasn't there any spring in the shoes? That's very strange," said Old Nick.

"No, there wasn't!" said the girl. "Why, my bark shoes are far better, and I can get on much faster in them than in these wretched things."

"You twist about as if you were dancing," said Old Nick; "but now I think you will have to dance away with me after all."

"Well, if you don't believe my words, I suppose you'll believe your eyes," she said. "Put on these grand shoes of yours, and try them yourself," she said, "and I'll put on my bark shoes, and then we'll have a race, so that you can see what they are good for," she said.

Well, that was reasonable enough, he thought, and, no doubt, he felt there was very little danger in trying it. So they agreed to race to the end of Lake Fryken and back, one on each side of the lake, which, as you know, is a very long one indeed. If she came in first she was to be free, but if she came in last she was to belong to him.

But the girl had to run home first of all, for she had a roll of cloth for the parson, which she must deliver before she tried her speed with Old Nick. Very well, that she might, for he went in fear of the parson; but the race should take place on the third day afterwards.

Now, as bad luck would have it for Old Nick, it so happened that the girl had a sister, who was so like her that it was impossible to know one from the other, for they were twins, the two girls.

But the sister was not mad about dancing, so Old Nick had not got scent of her. The girl now asked her sister to place herself at Frykstad, the south end of the lake, and she herself took up her position at Fryksend, the north end of it.

She had the bark shoes on, and Old Nick the leather ones; and so they set off, each on their side of the lake. The girl did not run very far, for she knew well enough how little running she need do; but Old Nick set off at full speed, much faster than one can ride on the railway.

But when he came to Frykstad he found the girl already there; and when he came back to Fryksend there she was too.

"Well, you see now?" said the girl.

"Of course I see," said Old Nick, but he was not the man to give in at once. "One time is no time, that you know," he said.

"Well, let's have another try," said the girl.

Yes, that he would, for the soles of his shoes were almost worn out, and then he knew what state the bark shoes would be in.

They set off for the second time, and Old Nick ran so fast that the air whistled round the corners of the houses in Sanne and Emtervik parishes; but when he came to Frykstad, the girl was already there, and when he got back to Fryksend, she was there before him this time also.

"Can you see now who comes in first?" she said.

"Yes, of course I can," said Old Nick, and began to dry the perspiration off his face, thinking all the time what a wonderful runner that girl must be. "But you know," he said, "twice is hardly half a time! It's the third time that counts."

"Let's have another try, then," said the girl.

Yes, that he would, for Old Nick is very sly, you know, for when the leather shoes were so torn to pieces that his feet were bleeding, he knew well enough what state the bark shoes would be in.

And so they set off again. Old Nick went at a terrible speed; it was just like a regular north-wester rushing past, for now he was furious. He rushed onwards, so that the roofs were swept away and the fences creaked and groaned all the way through Sanne and Emtervik parishes. But when he got to Frykstad the girl was there, and when he got back to Fryksend then she was there too.

His feet were now in such a plight that the flesh hung in pieces from them, and he was so out of breath, and groaned so hard, that the sound echoed in the mountains. The girl almost pitied the old creature, disgusting as he was.

"Do you see, now," she said, "that there's a better spring in my bark shoes than in your leather ones? There's nothing left of yours, while mine will hold out for another run, if you would like to try," she said.

No, Old Nick had now to acknowledge himself beaten, and so she was free.

"I've never seen the like of such a woman," he said; "but if you go on dancing and jumping about like that all your days we are sure to meet once more," he said.

"Oh, no!" said the girl. And since then she has never danced again, for it is not every time that you can succeed in getting away from Old Nick.

THE WAY of the WORLD

Norway

Once on a time there was a man who went into the wood to cut hop-poles, but he could find no trees so long and straight and slender as he wanted, till he came high up under a great heap of stones. There he heard groans and moans as though some one were at Death's door. So he went up to see who it was that needed help, and then he heard that the noise came from under a great flat stone which lay upon the heap. It was so heavy it would have taken many a man to lift it. But the man went down again into the wood and cut down a tree, which he turned into a lever, and with that he tilted up the stone, and lo! out from under it crawled a Dragon, and made at the man to swallow him up. But the man said he had saved the Dragon's life, and it was shameful thanklessness in him to want to eat him up.

"May be," said the Dragon, "but you might very well know I must be starved when I have been here hundreds of years and never tasted meat. Besides, it's the way of the world—that's how it pays its debts."

The man pleaded his cause stoutly, and begged prettily for his life; and at last they agreed to take the first living thing that came for a daysman, and if his doom went the other way the man should not lose his life, but if he said the same as the Dragon, the Dragon should eat the man.

The first thing that came was an old hound, who ran along the road down below under the hillside. Him they spoke to, and begged him to be judge.

"God knows," said the hound, "I have served my master truly ever since I was a little whelp. I have watched and watched many and many a night through while he lay warm asleep on his ear, and I have saved house and home from fire and thieves more than once; but now I can neither see nor hear any more, and he wants to shoot me. And so I must run away, and slink from house to house, and beg for my living till I die of hunger. No! it's the way of the world," said the hound; "that's how it pays its debts."

"Now I am coming to eat you up," said the Dragon, and tried to swallow the man again. But the man begged and prayed hard for his life, till they agreed to take the next comer for a judge; and if he said the same as the Dragon and the hound, the Dragon was to eat him, and get a meal of man's meat; but if he did not say so, the man was to get off with his life.

So there came an old horse limping down along the road which ran under the hill. Him they called out to come and settle the dispute. Yes; he was quite ready to do that.

"Now, I have served my master," said the horse, "as long as I could draw or carry. I have slaved and striven for him till the sweat trickled from every hair, and I have worked till I have grown lame, and halt, and worn out with toil and age; now I am fit for nothing. I am not worth my food, and so I am to have a bullet through me, he says. Nay! nay! It's the way of the world. That's how the world pays its debts."

"Well, now I'm coming to eat you," said the Dragon, who gaped wide, and wanted to swallow the man. But he begged again hard for his life.

But the Dragon said he must have a mouthful of man's meat; he was so hungry, he couldn't bear it any longer.

"See, yonder comes one who looks as if he was sent to be a judge between us," said the man, as he pointed to Reynard the fox, who came stealing between the stones of the heap.

"All good things are three," said the man; "let me ask him, too, and if he gives doom like the others, eat me up on the spot."

"Very well," said the Dragon. He, too, had heard that all good things were three, and so it should be a bargain. So the man talked to the fox as he had talked to the others.

"Yes, yes," said Reynard, "I see how it all is;" but as he said this he took the man a little on one side.

"What will you give me if I free you from the Dragon?" he whispered into the man's ear.

"You shall be free to come to my house, and to be lord and master over my hens and geese every Thursday night," said the man.

"Well, my dear Dragon," said Reynard, "this is a very hard nut to crack. I can't get it into my head how you, who are so big and mighty a beast, could find room to lie under yon stone."

"Can't you?" said the Dragon; "well, I lay under the hill-side, and sunned myself, and down came a landslip, and hurled the stone over me."

"All very likely, I dare say," said Reynard; "but still I can't understand it, and what's more I won't believe it till I see it."

So the man said they had better prove it, and the Dragon crawled down into his hole again; but in the twinkling of an eye they whipped out the lever, and down the stone crashed again on the Dragon.

"Lie now there till doomsday," said the fox. "You would eat the man, would you, who saved your life?"

The Dragon groaned, and moaned, and begged hard to come out; but the two went their way and left him alone.

The very first Thursday night Reynard came to be lord and master over the hen-roost, and hid himself behind a great pile of wood hard by. When the maid went to feed the fowls, in stole Reynard. She neither saw nor heard anything of him; but her back was scarce turned before he had sucked blood enough for a week, and stuffed himself so that he couldn't stir. So when she came again in the morning, there Reynard lay and snored, and slept in the morning sun, with all four legs stretched straight; and he was as sleek and round as a German sausage.

Away ran the lassie for the goody, and she came, and all the lasses with her, with sticks and brooms to beat Reynard; and, to tell the truth, they nearly banged the life out of him; but, just as it was almost all over with him, and he thought his last hour was come, he found a hole in the floor, and so he crept out, and limped and hobbled off to the wood.

"Oh, oh," said Reynard; "how true it is. 'Tis the way of the world; and this is how it pays its debts."

DEATH and the DOCTOR

Norway

Once on a time there was a lad who had lived as a servant a long time with a man of the North Country. This man was a master at ale-brewing; it was so out-of-the-way good the like of it was not to be found. So, when the lad was to leave his place and the man was to pay him the wages he had earned, he would take no other pay than a keg of Yule-ale. Well, he got it and set off with it, and he carried it both far and long, but the longer he carried the keg the heavier it got, and so he began to look about to see if any one were coming with whom he might have a drink, that the ale might lessen and the keg lighten. And after a long, long time, he met an old man with a big beard.

"Good day," said the man.

"Good day to you," said the lad.

"Whither away?" asked the man.

"I'm looking after some one to drink with, and get my keg lightened," said the lad.

"Can't you drink as well with me as with any one else?" said the man. "I have fared both far and wide, and I am both tired and thirsty."

"Well! why shouldn't I?" said the lad; "but tell me, whence do you come, and what sort of man are you?"

"I am 'Our Lord,' and come from Heaven," said the man.

"Thee will I not drink with," said the lad; "for thou makest such distinction between persons here in the world, and sharest rights so unevenly that some get so rich and some so poor. No! with thee I will not drink," and as he said this he trotted off with his keg again.

So when he had gone a bit farther the keg grew too heavy again; he thought he never could carry it any longer unless some one came with whom he might drink, and so lessen the ale in the keg. Yes! he met an ugly, scrawny man who came along fast and furious.

"Good day," said the man.

"Good day to you," said the lad.

"Whither away?" asked the man.

"Oh, I'm looking for some one to drink with, and get my keg lightened," said the lad.

"Can't you drink with me as well as with any one else?" said the man; "I have fared both far and wide, and I am tired and thirsty."

"Well, why not?" said the lad; "but who are you, and whence do you come?"

"Who am I? I am the De'il, and I come from Hell; that's where I come from," said the man.

"No!" said the lad; "thou only pinest and plaguest poor folk, and if there is any unhappiness astir, they always say it is thy fault. Thee I will not drink with."

So he went far and farther than far again with his ale-keg on his back, till he thought it grew so heavy there was no carrying it any farther. He began to look round again if any one were coming with whom he could drink and lighten his keg. So after a long, long time, another man came, and he was so dry and lean 'twas a wonder his bones hung together.

"Good day," said the man.

"Good day to you," said the lad.

"Whither away?" asked the man.

"Oh, I was only looking about to see if I could find some one to drink with, that my keg might be lightened a little, it is so heavy to carry."

"Can't you drink as well with me as with any one else?" said the man.

"Yes; why not?" said the lad. "But what sort of man are you?"

"They call me Death," said the man.

"The very man for my money," said the lad. "Thee I am glad to drink with," and as he said this he put down his keg, and began to tap the ale into a bowl. "Thou art an honest, trustworthy man, for thou treatest all alike, both rich and poor."

So he drank his health, and Death drank his health, and Death said he had never tasted such drink, and as the lad was fond of him, they drank bowl and bowl about, till the ale was lessened, and the keg grew light.

At last Death said, "I have never known drink which smacked better, or did me so much good as this ale that you have given me, and I scarce know what to give you in return." But, after he had thought awhile, he said the keg should never get empty, however much they drank out of it, and the ale that was in it should become a healing drink, by which the lad could make the sick whole again better than any doctor. And he also said that when the lad came into the sick man's room, Death would always be there, and show himself to him, and it should be to him for a sure token if he saw Death at the foot of the bed that he could cure the sick with a draught from the keg; but if he sat by the pillow, there was no healing nor medicine, for then the sick belonged to Death.

Well, the lad soon grew famous, and was called in far and near, and he helped many to health again who had been given over. When he came in and saw how Death sat by the sick man's bed, he foretold either life or death, and his foretelling was never wrong. He got both a rich and powerful man, and at last he was called in to a king's daughter far, far away in the world. She was so dangerously ill no doctor thought he could do her any good, and so they promised him all that he cared either to ask or have if he would only save her life.

Now, when he came into the princess's room, there sat Death at her pillow; but as he sat he dozed and nodded, and while he did this she felt herself better.

"Now, life or death is at stake," said the doctor; "and I fear, from what I see, there is no hope."

But they said he *must* save her, if it cost land and realm. So he looked at Death, and while he sat there and dozed again, he made a sign to the servants to turn the bed round so quickly that Death was left sitting at the foot, and at the very moment they turned the bed, the doctor gave her the draught, and her life was saved.

"Now you have cheated me," said Death, "and we are quits."

"I was forced to do it," said the doctor, "unless I wished to lose land and realm."

"That shan't help you much," said Death; "your time is up, for now you belong to me."

"Well," said the lad, "what must be must be; but you'll let me have time to read the Lord's Prayer first?"

Yes, he might have leave to do that; but he took very good care not to read the Lord's Prayer; everything else he read, but the Lord's Prayer never crossed his lips, and at last he thought he had cheated Death for good and all. But when Death thought he had really waited too long, he went to the lad's house one night, and hung up a great tablet with the Lord's Prayer painted on it over against his bed. So when the lad woke in the morning he began to read the tablet, and did not quite see what he was about till he came to Amen; but then it was just too late, and Death had him.

"ALL I POSSESS!"

Sweden

There was once a farmer who was so stingy and close fisted that he could scarcely find it in his heart to eat anything; and as for giving anything away to anybody, that was quite out of the question. He also wanted to accustom his wife to do without eating, but it fared with her as with the pedlar's mare; she died from an over-dose of that doctrine, and so he had to find another wife in her stead.

And although he was what he was, there were plenty of girls who made themselves agreeable to him and were willing to begin where his wife had left off. For you must know he was rich, the ugly fellow, and it was his money they were after, although they knew they would have to suffer a little in return.

But he was not satisfied with any of them, for if they ate ever so little, they were sure to want something to eat. Those who were stout and comely would be too expensive to keep, and those who were thin and slender were sure to have a big appetite; so he was not able to find any one to his liking, although he had been all over the parish looking for one.

But the lad on the farm came to his assistance. He had heard of a girl in one of the neighbouring parishes, who was not even able to eat as much as a whole pea at one meal, but made it do for two.

The farmer was glad to hear of this; she was the girl he would like to have, and although she was somewhat deaf, so that she never heard more than half of what people said to her, he lost no time in proposing to the girl. Her father and mother said yes at once, seeing that the suitor was so rich, and it did not take him long to persuade the girl herself. A husband she must have some time or other, and so they clinched the matter, and the farmer entered into wedlock for the second time.

But after a time he began to wonder how his wife really managed to keep alive, for he noticed that she never took a morsel of food, or even drank so much as a drop of water, and this he thought was altogether too little. But she seemed to thrive very well for all that, and he even thought she was getting a little stouter.

"I wonder if she's deceiving me?" he thought.

So one day, when he was driving home from his work in the fields, he happened to meet his wife, who was coming from the cowshed with the milk.

"I wonder if she doesn't take a sip of the milk when she is straining it," he thought, and so he asked the lad to help him up on the roof and pull the damper aside, for he wanted to look down the chimney and see what his wife was doing. And this he did. He climbed up on the roof and put his head down the chimney, peering and prying all he could.

The lad then went in to his mistress.

"Master is now looking down the chimney," he said.

"Down the chimney?" said the wife. "Well, then you must put some faggots on the hearth and make a fire."

"I daren't," said the lad.

"If you daren't, I dare," said the woman, and so she made a fire and blew into it.

The farmer began shouting, for the smoke was nearly suffocating him.

"Bless me, is that you, husband?" said his wife.

"Yes, of course it is," said the farmer.

"What are you hanging there for?" she said.

"Oh, I was longing so much for you, wifey, that I went the shortest way," he said, and then he fell down on the hearth, and burned himself a good deal.

Some days passed and his wife neither ate nor drank, but if she did not grow stouter she did not become thinner.

"I wonder if she doesn't eat some of the bacon when she goes to the storehouse," he thought; and so he stole into the storehouse and ripped up one end of a large feather bed which was lying there. He crept into it and asked the lad to sew the ticking together again.

The lad did as he was bid, and then he went in to his mistress.

"Master is now lying inside the feather bed in the storehouse," he said.

"Inside the feather bed in the storehouse?" said the wife. "You must go and beat it well, so that neither dust nor moths get into it," she said, and so she took down a couple of stout hazel sticks and gave them to the lad.

"I daren't," said the lad.

"If you daren't, I dare," said the wife, and she went to the storehouse and began to beat the feather bed with all her might, so that the feathers flew about, and the farmer began shouting, for the blows hit him right across his face.

"Bless me, is that you, husband?" said the woman.

"Yes, of course it is," said the farmer.

"What are you lying there for?" said his wife.

"I thought I would lie on something better than straw for once," said the husband. They then ripped open the feather bed, and when he came out the blood was still streaming down his face.

Some days then passed and the wife neither ate nor drank, but her husband thought she was growing still stouter and more cheerful than ever.

"The devil knows what's at the bottom of all this," he thought. "I wonder if she drinks the beer when she goes into the cellar?"

And so he went down into the cellar and knocked the bottom out of an empty beer-barrel, and then he crept into the barrel, and asked the lad to put the bottom in again. The lad did as he was bid, and then he went in to his mistress.

"Master is now lying in the beer-barrel in the cellar," said the lad.

"In the beer-barrel in the cellar?" said the wife. "You must fill it with boiling juniper lye, for it's getting sour and leaky," she said.

"I daren't," said the lad.

"If you daren't, I dare," said the wife, and so she began boiling juniper lye, and then she poured it into the barrel. The farmer began to shout, but she poured a whole kettleful into the barrel, and yet another after that.

The man went on shouting louder and louder.

"Bless me, is that you, husband?" said the wife.

"Yes, of course it is," yelled the farmer.

"What are you lying there for?" said his wife.

But the farmer was not able to give any answer. He only moaned and groaned, for he was terribly scalded, and when they got him out of the barrel he was more dead than alive, and they had to carry him to his bed.

He now wished to see the parson, and while the lad went to fetch him the wife began to prepare some tasty dishes and to make cheese cakes and other nice things for the parson, so that he should not go away with an empty stomach.

But when the farmer saw how lavish she was in preparing all the dishes he shouted still louder than when he was scalded:

"All I possess! All I possess!" he cried, for he now believed they were going to eat up everything he had, and he knew that both the parson and the clerk were people who could make themselves at home and make a clean sweep of the table.

When the parson arrived the farmer was still shouting:

"All I possess! All I possess!"

"What is it your husband is saying?" said the parson.

"Oh, my husband is so terribly good and kind," said the wife. "He means that I shall have all he possesses," she said.

"His words must then be considered and looked upon as an intimation of his last will and testament," said the parson.

"Just so!" said the wife.

"All I possess! All I possess!" cried the farmer, and then he died.

His wife then had him buried, and afterwards she went to the proper authorities about her husband's affairs. And as both the parson and the clerk could give evidence that the farmer's last words were that she should have all he possessed she got it all. And when a year was gone she married the lad on the farm, but whether after that time she was just as hard of hearing I have never heard.

THE OLD WOMAN
and the TRAMP

Sweden

There was once a tramp, who went plodding his way through a forest. The distance between the houses was so great that he had little hope of finding a shelter before the night set in. But all of a sudden he saw some lights between the trees. He then discovered a cottage, where there was a fire burning on the hearth. How nice it would be to roast one's self before that fire, and to get a bite of something, he thought; and so he dragged himself towards the cottage.

Just then an old woman came towards him.

"Good evening, and well met!" said the tramp.

"Good evening," said the woman. "Where do you come from?"

"South of the sun, and east of the moon," said the tramp; "and now I am on the way home again, for I have been all over the world with the exception of this parish," he said.

"You must be a great traveller, then," said the woman. "What may be your business here?"

"Oh, I want a shelter for the night," he said.

"I thought as much," said the woman; "but you may as well get away from here at once, for my husband is not at home, and my place is not an inn," she said.

"My good woman," said the tramp, "you must not be so cross and hard-hearted, for we are both human beings, and should help one another, it is written."

"Help one another?" said the woman, "help? Did you ever hear such a thing? Who'll help me, do you think? I haven't got a morsel in the house! No, you'll have to look for quarters elsewhere," she said.

But the tramp was like the rest of his kind; he did not consider himself beaten at the first rebuff. Although the old woman grumbled and complained as much as she could, he was just as persistent as ever, and went on begging and praying like a starved dog, until at last she gave in, and he got permission to lie on the floor for the night.

That was very kind, he thought, and he thanked her for it.

"Better on the floor without sleep, than suffer cold in the forest deep," he said; for he was a merry fellow, this tramp, and was always ready with a rhyme.

When he came into the room he could see that the woman was not so badly off as she had pretended; but she was a greedy and stingy woman of the worst sort, and was always complaining and grumbling.

He now made himself very agreeable, of course, and asked her in his most insinuating manner for something to eat.

"Where am I to get it from?" said the woman. "I haven't tasted a morsel myself the whole day."

But the tramp was a cunning fellow, he was.

"Poor old granny, you must be starving," he said. "Well, well, I suppose I shall have to ask you to have something with me, then."

"Have something with you!" said the woman. "You don't look as if you could ask any one to have anything! What have you got to offer one, I should like to know?"

"He who far and wide does roam sees many things not known at home; and he who many things has seen has wits about him and senses keen," said the tramp. "Better dead than lose one's head! Lend me a pot, granny!"

The old woman now became very inquisitive, as you may guess, and so she let him have a pot.

He filled it with water and put it on the fire, and then he blew with all his might till the fire was burning fiercely all round it. Then he took a four-inch nail from his pocket, turned it three times in his hand and put it into the pot.

The woman stared with all her might.

"What's this going to be?" she asked.

"Nail broth," said the tramp, and began to stir the water with the porridge stick.

"Nail broth?" asked the woman.

"Yes, nail broth," said the tramp.

The old woman had seen and heard a good deal in her time, but that anybody could have made broth with a nail, well, she had never heard the like before.

"That's something for poor people to know," she said, "and I should like to learn how to make it."

"That which is not worth having, will always go a-begging," said the tramp.

But if she wanted to learn how to make it she had only to watch him, he said, and went on stirring the broth.

The old woman squatted on the ground, her hands clasping her knees, and her eyes following his hand as he stirred the broth.

"This generally makes good broth," he said; "but this time it will very likely be rather thin, for I have been making broth the whole week with the same nail. If one only had a handful of sifted oatmeal to put in, that would make it all right," he said. "But what one has to go without, it's no use thinking more about," and so he stirred the broth again.

"Well, I think I have a scrap of flour somewhere," said the old woman, and went out to fetch some, and it was both good and fine.

The tramp began putting the flour into the broth, and went on stirring, while the woman sat staring now at him and then at the pot until her eyes nearly burst their sockets.

"This broth would be good enough for company," he said, putting in one handful of flour after another. "If I had only a bit of salted beef and a few potatoes to put in, it would be fit for gentlefolks, however particular they might be," he said. "But what one has to go without, it's no use thinking more about."

When the old woman really began to think it over, she thought she had some potatoes, and perhaps a bit of beef as well; and these she gave the tramp, who went on stirring, while she sat and stared as hard as ever.

"This will be grand enough for the best in the land," he said.

"Well, I never!" said the woman; "and just fancy—all with a nail!"

He was really a wonderful man, that tramp! He could do more than drink a sup and turn the tankard up, he could.

"If one had only a little barley and a drop of milk, we could ask the king himself to have some of it," he said; "for this is what he has every blessed evening—that I know, for I have been in service under the king's cook," he said.

"Dear me! Ask the king to have some! Well, I never!" exclaimed the woman, slapping her knees.

She was quite awestruck at the tramp and his grand connections.

"But what one has to go without, it's no use thinking more about," said the tramp.

And then she remembered she had a little barley; and as for milk, well, she wasn't quite out of that, she said, for her best cow had just calved. And then she went to fetch both the one and the other.

The tramp went on stirring, and the woman sat staring, one moment at him and the next at the pot.

Then all at once the tramp took out the nail.

"Now it's ready, and now we'll have a real good feast," he said. "But to this kind of soup the king and the queen always take a dram or two, and one sandwich at least. And then they always have a cloth on the table when they eat," he said. "But what one has to go without, it's no use thinking more about."

But by this time the old woman herself had begun to feel quite grand and fine, I can tell you; and if that was all that was wanted to make it just as the king had it, she thought it would be nice to have it just the same way for once, and play at being king and queen with the tramp. She went straight to a cupboard and brought out the brandy bottle, dram glasses, butter and cheese, smoked beef and veal, until at last the table looked as if it were decked out for company.

Never in her life had the old woman had such a grand feast, and never had she tasted such broth, and just fancy, made only with a nail!

She was in such a good and merry humour at having learnt such an economical way of making broth that she did not know how to make enough of the tramp who had taught her such a useful thing.

So they ate and drank, and drank and ate, until they became both tired and sleepy.

The tramp was now going to lie down on the floor. But that would never do, thought the old woman; no, that was impossible. "Such a grand person must have a bed to lie in," she said.

He did not need much pressing. "It's just like the sweet Christmas time," he said, "and a nicer woman I never came across. Ah, well! Happy are they who meet with such good people," said he; and he lay down on the bed and went asleep.

And next morning when he woke the first thing he got was coffee and a dram.

When he was going the old woman gave him a bright dollar piece.

"And thanks, many thanks, for what you have taught me," she said. "Now I shall live in comfort, since I have learnt how to make broth with a nail."

"Well, it isn't very difficult, if one only has something good to add to it," said the tramp as he went his way.

The woman stood at the door staring after him.

"Such people don't grow on every bush," she said.

JOURNEYS

THE HONEST PENNY

Norway

Once on a time there was a poor woman who lived in a tumble-down hut far away in the wood. Little had she to eat, and nothing at all to burn, and so she sent a little boy she had out into the wood to gather fuel. He ran and jumped, and jumped and ran, to keep himself warm, for it was a cold grey autumn day, and every time he found a bough or a root for his billet, he had to beat his arms across his breast, for his fists were as red as the cranberries over which he walked, for very cold. So when he had got his billet of wood and was off home, he came upon a clearing of stumps on the hillside, and there he saw a white crooked stone.

"Ah! you poor old stone," said the boy; "how white and wan you are! I'll be bound you are frozen to death;" and with that he took off his jacket and laid it on the stone. So when he got home with his billet of wood his mother asked what it all meant that he walked about in wintry weather in his shirt-sleeves. Then he told her how he had seen an old crooked stone which was all white and wan for frost, and how he had given it his jacket.

"What a fool you are!" said his mother; "do you think a stone can freeze? But even if it froze till it shook again, know this—every one is nearest to his own self. It costs quite enough to get clothes to your back, without your going and hanging them on stones in the clearings;" and as she said that, she hunted the boy out of the house to fetch his jacket.

So when he came where the stone stood, lo! it had turned itself and lifted itself up on one side from the ground. "Yes! yes! this is since you got the jacket, poor old thing," said the boy.

But when he looked a little closer at the stone, he saw a money-box, full of bright silver, under it.

"This is stolen money, no doubt," thought the boy; "no one puts money, come by honestly, under a stone away in the wood."

So he took the money-box and bore it down to a tarn hard by and threw the whole hoard into the tarn; but one silver penny-piece floated on the top of the water.

"Ah! ah! that is honest," said the lad; "for what is honest never sinks."

So he took the silver penny and went home with it and his jacket. Then he told his mother how it had all happened, how the stone had turned itself, and how he had found a money-box full of silver money, which he had thrown out into the tarn because it was stolen money, and how one silver penny floated on the top.

"That I took," said the boy, "because it was honest."

"You are a born fool," said his mother, for she was very angry; "were naught else honest than what floats on water, there wouldn't be much honesty in the world. And even though the money were stolen ten times over, still you had found it; and I tell you again what I told you before, everyone is nearest to his own self. Had you only taken that money we might have lived well and happy all our days. But a ne'er-do-weel thou art, and a ne'er-do-weel thou wilt be, and now I won't drag on any longer toiling and moiling for thee. Be off with thee into the world and earn thine own bread."

So the lad had to go out into the wide world, and he went both far and long seeking a place. But wherever he came, folk thought him too little and weak, and said they could put him to no use. At last he came to a merchant, and there he got leave to be in the kitchen and carry in wood and water for the cook. Well, after he had been there a long time, the merchant had to make a journey into foreign lands, and so he asked all his servants what he should buy and bring home for each of them. So, when all had said what they would have, the turn came to the scullion too, who brought in wood and water for the cook. Then he held out his penny.

"Well, what shall I buy with this?" asked the merchant; "there won't be much time lost over this bargain."

"Buy what I can get for it. It is honest, that I know," said the lad.

That his master gave his word to do, and so he sailed away.

So when the merchant had unladed his ship and laded her again in foreign lands, and bought what he had promised his servants to buy, he came down to his ship, and was just going to shove off from the wharf. Then all at once it came into his head that the scullion had sent out a silver penny with him, that he might buy something for him.

"Must I go all the way back to the town for the sake of a silver penny? One would then have small gain in taking such a beggar into one's house," thought the merchant.

Just then an old wife came walking by with a bag at her back.

"What have you got in your bag, mother?" asked the merchant.

"Oh! nothing else than a cat. I can't afford to feed it any longer, so I thought I would throw it into the sea, and make away with it," answered the woman.

Then the merchant said to himself, "Didn't the lad say I was to buy what I could get for his penny?" So he asked the old wife if she would take four farthings for her cat. Yes! the goody was not slow to say "done," and so the bargain was soon struck.

Now when the merchant had sailed a bit, fearful weather fell on him, and such a storm, there was nothing for it but to drive and drive till he did not know whither he was going. At last he came to a land on which he had never set foot before, and so up he went into the town.

At the inn where he turned in, the board was laid with a rod for each man who sat at it. The merchant thought it very strange, for he couldn't at all make out what they were to do with all these rods; but he sat him down, and thought he would watch well what the others did, and do like them. Well! as soon as the meat was set on the board, he saw well enough what the rods meant; for out swarmed mice in thousands, and each one who sat at the board had to take to his rod and flog and flap about him, and naught else could be heard than one cut of the rod harder than the one which went before it. Sometimes they whipped one another in the face, and just gave themselves time to say, "Beg pardon," and then at it again.

"Hard work to dine in this land!" said the merchant. "But don't folk keep cats here?"

"Cats?" they all asked, for they did not know what cats were.

So the merchant sent and fetched the cat he had bought for the scullion, and as soon as the cat got on the table, off ran the mice to their holes, and folks had never in the memory of man had such rest at their meat.

Then they begged and prayed the merchant to sell them the cat, and at last, after a long, long time, he promised to let them have it; but he would have a hundred dollars for it; and that sum they gave and thanks besides.

So the merchant sailed off again; but he had scarce got good sea-room before he saw the cat sitting up at the mainmast head, and all at once again came foul weather and a storm worse than the first, and he drove and drove till he got to a country where he had never been before. The merchant went up to an inn, and here, too, the board was spread with rods; but they were much bigger and longer than the first. And, to tell the truth, they had need to be; for here the mice were many more, and every mouse was twice as big as those he had before seen.

So he sold the cat again, and this time he got two hundred dollars for it, and that without any haggling.

So when he had sailed away from that land and got a bit out at sea, there sat Grimalkin again at the masthead; and the bad weather began at once again, and the end of it was, he was again driven to a land where he had never been before.

He went ashore, up to the town, and turned into an inn. There, too, the board was laid with rods, but every rod was an ell and a half long, and as thick as a small broom; and the folk said that to sit at meat was the hardest trial they had, for there were thousands of big ugly rats, so that it was only with sore toil and trouble one could get a morsel into one's mouth, 'twas such hard work to keep off the rats. So the cat had to be fetched up from the ship once more, and then folks got their food in peace. Then they all begged and prayed the merchant, for heaven's sake, to sell them his cat. For a long time he said "No;" but at last he gave his word to take three hundred dollars for it. That sum they paid down at once, and thanked him and blessed him for it into the bargain.

Now, when the merchant got out to sea, he fell a-thinking how much the lad had made out of the penny he had sent out with him.

"Yes, yes, some of the money he shall have," said the merchant to himself, "but not all. Me it is that he has to thank for the cat I bought; and besides, every man is nearest to his own self."

But as soon as ever the merchant thought this, such a storm and gale arose that everyone thought the ship must founder. So the merchant saw there was no help for it, and he had to vow that the lad should have every penny; and no sooner had he vowed this vow, than the weather turned good, and he got a snoring breeze fair for home.

So, when he got to land, he gave the lad the six hundred dollars, and his daughter besides; for now the little scullion was just as rich as his master, the merchant, and even richer; and, after that, the lad lived all his days in mirth and jollity; and he sent for his mother, and treated her as well as or better than he treated himself; "for," said the lad, "I don't think that everyone is nearest to his own self."

THE BOY WHO DID NOT KNOW WHAT FEAR WAS

Iceland

There was once a boy so courageous and spirited that his relations despaired of ever frightening him into obedience to their will, and took him to the parish priest to be brought up. But the priest could not subdue him in the least, though the boy never showed either obstinacy or ill-temper towards him.

Once in the winter three dead bodies were brought to be buried, but as it was late in the afternoon they were put into the church till next day, when the priest would be able to bury them. In those days it was the custom to bury people without coffins, and only wrapped up in grave-clothes. The priest ordered these three bodies to be laid a little distance apart, across the middle of the church.

After nightfall the priest said to the boy, "Run into the church and fetch me the book which I left on the altar."

With his usual willingness he ran into the church, which was quite dark, and half way to the altar stumbled against something which lay on the floor, and fell down on his face. Not in the least alarmed, he got up again, and, after groping about, found that he had stumbled over one of the corpses, which he took in his arms and pushed into the side-benches out of his way. He tumbled over the other two, and disposed of them in like manner. Then, taking the book from the altar, he left the church, shut the door behind him, and gave the volume to the priest, who asked him if he had encountered anything extraordinary in the church.

"Not that I can remember," said the boy.

The priest asked again, "Did you not find three corpses lying across your passage?"

"Oh yes," replied he, "but what about them?"

"Did they not lie in your way?"

"Yes, but they did not hinder me."

The priest asked, "How did you get to the altar?"

The boy replied, "I stuck the good folk into the side-benches, where they lie quietly enough."

The priest shook his head, but said nothing more that night.

Next morning he said to the boy, "You must leave me; I cannot keep near me any longer one who is shameless enough to break the repose of the dead."

The boy, nothing loth, bade farewell to the priest and his family, and wandered about some little time without a home.

Once he came to a cottage, where he slept the night, and there the people told him that the Bishop of Skálholt was just dead. So next day he went off to Skálholt, and arriving there in the evening, begged a night's lodging.

The people said to him, "You may have it and welcome, but you must take care of yourself."

"Why take care of myself so much?" asked the lad.

They told him that after the death of the bishop, no one could stay in the house after nightfall, as some ghost or goblin walked about there, and that on this account everyone had to leave the place after twilight.

The boy answered, "Well and good; that will just suit me."

At twilight the people all left the place, taking leave of the boy, whom they did not expect to see again alive.

When they had all gone, the boy lighted a candle and examined every room in the house till he came to the kitchen, where he found large quantities of smoked mutton hung up to the rafters. So, as he had not tasted meat for some time, and had a capital appetite, he cut some of the dried mutton off with his knife, and placing a pot on the fire, which was still burning, cooked it.

When he had finished cutting up the meat, and had put the lid on the pot, he heard a voice from the top of the chimney, which said, "May I come down?"

The lad answered, "Yes, why not?"

Then there fell down on to the floor of the kitchen half a giant,—head, arms, hands, and body, as far as the waist, and lay there motionless.

After this he heard another voice from the chimney, saying, "May I come down?"

"If you like," said the boy; "why not?"

Accordingly down came another part of the giant, from the waist to the thighs, and lay on the floor motionless.

Then he heard a third voice from the same direction, which said, "May I come down?"

"Of course," he replied; "you must have something to stand upon."

So a huge pair of legs and feet came down and lay by the rest of the body, motionless.

After a bit the boy, finding this want of movement rather tedious, said, "Since you have contrived to get yourself all in, you had better get up and go away."

Upon this the pieces crept together, and the giant rose on his feet from the floor, and, without uttering a word, stalked out of the kitchen. The lad followed him, till they came to a large hall, in which stood a wooden chest. This chest the goblin opened, and the lad saw that it was full of money. Then the goblin took the money out in handfuls, and poured it like water over his head, till the floor was covered with heaps of it; and, having spent half the night thus, spent the other half in restoring the gold to the chest in the like manner. The boy stood by and watched him filling the chest again, and gathering all the stray coins together by sweeping his great arms violently over the floor, as if he dreaded to be interrupted before he could get them all in, which the lad fancied must be because the day was approaching.

When the goblin had shut up the coffer, he rushed past the lad as if to get out of the hall; but the latter said to him, "Do not be in too great a hurry."

"I must make haste," replied the other, "for the day is dawning."

But the boy took him by the sleeve and begged him to remain yet a little longer for friendship's sake.

At this the goblin waxed angry, and, clutching hold of the youth, said, "Now you shall delay me no longer."

But the latter clung tight to him, and slipped out of the way of every blow he dealt, and some time passed away in this kind of struggle. It happened, however, at last, that the giant turned his back to the open door, and the boy, seeing his chance, tripped him up and butted at him with his head, so that the other fell heavily backwards, half in and half out of the hall, and broke his spine upon the threshold. At the same moment the first ray of dawn struck his eyes through the open house door, and he instantly sank into the ground in two pieces, one each side of the door of the hall. Then the courageous boy, though half dead from fatigue, made two crosses of wood and drove them into the ground where the two parts of the goblin had disappeared. This done, he fell asleep till, when the sun was well up, the people came back to Skálholt. They were amazed and rejoiced to find him still alive, asking him whether he had seen anything in the night.

"Nothing out of the common," he said.

So he stayed there all that day, both because he was tired, and because the people were loth to let him go.

In the evening, when the people began as usual to leave the place, he begged them to stay, assuring them that they would be troubled by neither ghost nor goblin. But in spite of his assurances they insisted upon going, though they left him this time without any fear for his safety. When they were gone, he went to bed and slept soundly till morning.

On the return of the people he told them all about his struggle with the goblin, showed them the crosses he had set up, and the chestful of money in the hall, and assured them that they would never again be troubled at night, so need not leave the place. They thanked him most heartily for his spirit and courage, and asked him to name any reward he would like to receive, whether money or other precious things, inviting him, in addition, to remain with them as long as ever he chose. He was grateful for their offers, but said, "I do not care for money, nor can I make up my mind to stay longer with you."

Next day he addressed himself to his journey, and no persuasion could induce him to remain at Skálholt. For he said, "I have no more business here, as you can now, without fear, live in the bishop's house." And taking leave of them all, he directed his steps northwards, into the wilderness.

For a long time nothing new befell him, until one day he came to a large cave, into which he entered. In a smaller cave within the other he found twelve beds, all in disorder and unmade. As it was yet early, he thought he could do no better than employ himself in making them, and having made them, threw himself on to the one nearest the entrance, covered himself up, and went to sleep.

After a little while he awoke and heard the voices of men talking in the cave, and wondering who had made the beds for them, saying that, whoever he was, they were much obliged to him for his pains. He saw, on looking out, that they were twelve armed men of noble aspect. When they had had supper, they came into the inner cave and eleven of them went to bed. But the twelfth man, whose bed was next to the entrance, found the boy in it, and called to the others. They rose and thanked the lad for having made their beds for them, and begged him to remain with them as their servant, for they said that they never found time to do any work for themselves, as they were compelled to go out every day at sunrise to fight their enemies, and never returned till night. The lad asked them why they were forced to fight day after day? They answered that they had over and over again fought, and overcome their enemies, but that though they killed them over-night they always came to life again before morning, and would come to the cave and slay them all in their beds if they were not up and ready on the field at sunrise.

In the morning the cave-men went out fully armed, leaving the lad behind to look after the household work.

About noon he went in the same direction as the men had taken, in order to find out where the battle-field was, and as soon as he had espied it in the distance, ran back to the cave.

In the evening the warriors returned weary and dispirited, but were glad to find that the boy had arranged everything for them, so that they had nothing more to do than eat their supper and go to bed.

When they were all asleep, the boy wondered to himself how it could possibly come to pass that their enemies rose every night from the dead. So moved with curiosity was he, that as soon as he was sure that his companions were fast asleep he took what of their weapons and armour he found to fit him best, and stealing out of the cave, made off in the direction of the battle-field. There was nothing at first to be seen there but corpses and trunkless heads, so he waited a little time to see what would happen. About dawn he perceived a mound near him open of itself, and an old woman in a blue cloak come out with a glass phial in her hand. He noticed her go up to a dead warrior, and having picked up his head, smear his neck with some ointment out of the phial and place the head and trunk together. Instantly the warrior stood erect, a living man. The hag repeated this to two or three, until the boy seeing now the secret of the thing, rushed up to her and stabbed her to death as well as the men she had raised, who were yet stupid and heavy as if after sleep. Then taking the phial, he tried whether he could revive the corpses with the ointment, and found on experiment that he could do so success-fully. So he amused himself for a while in reviving the men and killing them again, till, at sunrise, his companions arrived on the field.

They were mightily astonished to see him there, and told him that they had missed him as well as some of their weapons and armour; but they were rejoiced to find their enemies lying dead on the field instead of being alive and awaiting them in battle array, and asked the lad how he had got the idea of thus going at night to the battle-field, and what he had done.

He told them all that had passed, showed them the phial of ointment, and, in order to prove its power, smeared the neck of one of the corpses, who at once rose to his feet, but was instantly killed again by the cave-men. They thanked the boy heartily for the service he had rendered them, and begged him to remain among them, offering him at the same time money for his work. He declared that he was quite willing, paid or unpaid, to stay with them, as long as they liked to keep him. The cave-men were well pleased with his answer, and having embraced the lad, set to work to strip their enemies of their weapons: made a heap of them with the old woman on the top, and burned them; and then, going into the mound, appro-priated to themselves all the treasures they found there. After this they proposed the game of killing each other, to try how it was to die, as they could restore one another to life again. So they killed each other, but by smearing themselves with the ointment, they at once returned to life.

Now this was great sport for a while.

But once, when they had cut off the head of the lad, they put it on again wrong-side before. And as the lad saw himself behind, he became as if mad with fright, and begged the men to release him by all means from such a painful sight.

But when the cave-folk had run to him and, cutting off his head, placed it on all right again, he came back to his full senses, and was as fearless as ever before.

The boy lived with them ever afterwards, and no more stories are told about him.

THE TRUE BRIDE:
THE STORY of ILONA
and the KING'S SON

Finland

There were once two orphans, a brother and a sister, who lived alone in the old farmhouse where their fathers before them had lived for many generations. The brother's name was Osmo, the sister's Ilona. Osmo was an industrious youth, but the farm was small and barren and he was hard put to it to make a livelihood.

"Sister," he said one day, "I think it might be well if I went out into the world and found work."

"Do as you think best, brother," Ilona said. "I'm sure I can manage on here alone."

So Osmo started off, promising to come back for his sister as soon as he could give her a new home. He wandered far and wide and at last got employment from the King's Son as a shepherd.

The King's Son was about Osmo's age, and often when he met Osmo tending his flocks he would stop and talk to him.

One day Osmo told the King's Son about his sister, Ilona.

"I have wandered far over the face of the earth," he said, "and never have I seen so beautiful a maiden as Ilona."

"What does she look like?" the King's Son asked.

Osmo drew a picture of her and she seemed to the King's Son so beautiful that at once he fell in love with her.

"Osmo," he said, "if you will go home and get your sister, I will marry her."

So Osmo hurried home not by the long land route by which he had come but straight over the water in a boat.

"Sister," he cried, as soon as he saw Ilona, "you must come with me at once for the King's Son wishes to marry you!"

He thought Ilona would be overjoyed, but she sighed and shook her head.

"What is it, sister? Why do you sigh?"

"Because it grieves me to leave this old house where our fathers have lived for so many generations."

"Nonsense, Ilona! What is this little old house compared to the King's castle where you will live once you marry the King's Son!"

But Ilona only shook her head.

"It's no use, brother! I can't bear to leave this old house until the grindstone with which our fathers for generations ground their meal is worn out."

When Osmo found she was firm, he went secretly and broke the old grindstone into small pieces. He then put the pieces together so that the stone looked the same as before. But of course the next time Ilona touched it, it fell apart.

"Now, sister, you'll come, will you not?" Osmo asked.

But again Ilona shook her head.

"It's no use, brother. I can't bear to go until the old stool where our mothers have sat spinning these many generations is worn through."

So again Osmo took things into his own hands and going secretly to the old spinning stool he broke it and when Ilona sat on it again it fell to pieces.

Then Ilona said she couldn't go until the old mortar which had been in use for generations should fall to bits at a blow from the pestle. Osmo cracked the mortar and the next time Ilona struck it with the pestle it broke.

Then Ilona said she couldn't go until the old worn doorsill over which so many of their forefathers had walked should fall to splinters at the brush of her skirts. So Osmo secretly split the old doorsill into thin slivers and, when next Ilona stepped over it, the brush of her skirts sent the splinters flying.

"I see now I must go," Ilona said, "for the house of our forefathers no longer holds me."

So she packed all her ribbons and her bodices and skirts in a bright wooden box and, calling her little dog Pilka, she stepped into the boat and Osmo rowed her off in the direction of the King's castle.

Soon they passed a long narrow spit of land at the end of which stood a woman waving her arms. That is she looked like a woman. Really she was Suyettar[1] but they, of course, did not know this.

"Take me in your boat!" she cried.

"Shall we?" Osmo asked his sister.

"I don't think we ought to," Ilona said. "We don't know who she is or what she wants and she may be evil."

So Osmo rowed on. But the woman kept shouting:

"Hi, there! Take me in your boat! Take me!"

A second time Osmo paused and asked his sister:

"Don't you think we ought to take her?"

"No," Ilona said.

So Osmo rowed on again. At this the creature raised such a pitiful outcry demanding what they meant denying assistance to a poor woman that Osmo was unable longer to refuse and in spite of Ilona's warning he rowed to land.

Suyettar instantly jumped into the boat and seated herself in the middle with her face towards Osmo and her back towards Ilona.

"What a fine young man!" Suyettar said in whining flattering tones. "See how strong he is at the oars! And what a beautiful girl, too! I daresay the King's Son would fall in love with her if ever he saw her!"

Thereupon Osmo very foolishly told Suyettar that the King's Son had already promised to marry Ilona. At that an evil look came into Suyettar's face and she sat silent for a time biting her fingers. Then she began mumbling a spell that made Osmo deaf to what Ilona was saying and Ilona deaf to what Osmo was saying.

At last in the distance the towers of the King's castle appeared.

"Stand up, sister!" Osmo said. "Shake out your skirts and arrange your pretty ribbons! We'll soon be landing now!"

Ilona could see her brother's lips moving but of course she could not hear what he was saying.

---

1.   A transliteration of Syöjätär, the name of the dread Finnish witch.

"What is it, brother?" she asked.

Suyettar answered for him:

"Osmo orders you to jump headlong into the water!"

"No! No!" Ilona cried. "He couldn't order anything so cruel as that!"

Presently Osmo said:

"Sister, what ails you? Don't you hear me? Shake out your skirts and arrange your pretty ribbons for we'll soon be landing now."

"What is it, brother?" Ilona asked.

As before Suyettar answered for him:

"Osmo orders you to jump headlong into the water!"

"Brother, how can you order so cruel a thing!" Ilona cried, bursting into tears. "Is it for this you made me leave the home of my fathers?"

A third time Osmo said:

"Stand up, sister, and shake out your skirts and arrange your ribbons! We'll soon be landing now!"

"I can't hear you, brother! What is it you say?"

Suyettar turned on her fiercely and screamed:

"Osmo orders you to jump headlong into the water!"

"If he says I must, I must!" poor Ilona sobbed, and with that she leapt overboard.

Osmo tried to save her but Suyettar held him back and with her own arms rowed off and Ilona was left to sink.

"What will become of me now!" Osmo cried. "When the King's Son finds I have not brought him my sister he will surely order my death!"

"Not at all!" Suyettar said. "Do as I say and no harm will come to you. Offer me to the King's Son and tell him I am your sister. He won't know the difference and anyway I'm sure I'm just as beautiful as Ilona ever was!"

With that Suyettar opened the wooden box that held Ilona's clothes and helped herself to skirt and bodice and gay colored ribbons. She decked herself out in these and for a little while she really did succeed in looking like a pretty young girl.

So Osmo presented Suyettar to the King's Son as Ilona, and the King's Son because he had given his word married her. But before one day was past, he called Osmo to him and asked him angrily:

"What did you mean by telling me your sister was beautiful?"

"Isn't she beautiful?" Osmo faltered.

"No! I thought she was at first but she isn't! She is ugly and evil and you shall pay the penalty for having deceived me!"

Thereupon he ordered that Osmo be shut up in a place filled with serpents.

"If you are innocent," the King's Son said, "the serpents will not harm you. If you are guilty they will devour you!"

Meanwhile poor Ilona when she jumped into the water sank down, down, down, until she reached the Sea King's palace. They received her kindly there and comforted her and the Sea King's Son, touched by her grief and beauty, offered to marry her. But Ilona was homesick for the upper world and would not listen to him.

"I want to see my brother again!" she wept.

They told her that the King's Son had thrown her brother to the serpents and had married Suyettar in her stead, but Ilona still begged so pitifully to be allowed to return to earth that at last the Sea King said:

"Very well, then! For three successive nights I will allow you to return to the upper world. But after that never again!"

So they decked Ilona in the lovely jewels of the sea with great strands of pearls about her neck and to each of her ankles they attached long silver chains. As she rose in the water the sound of the chains was like the chiming of silver bells and could be heard for five miles.

Ilona came to the surface of the water just where Osmo had landed. The first thing she saw was his boat at the water's edge and curled up asleep in the bottom of the boat her own little dog, Pilka.

"Pilka!" Ilona cried, and the little dog woke with a bark of joy and licked Ilona's hand and yelped and frisked.

Then Ilona sang this magic song to Pilka:

> "Peely, peely, Pilka, pide,
> Lift the latch and slip inside!
> Past the watchdog in the yard,
> Past the sleeping men on guard!
> Creep in softly as a snake,

Then creep out before they wake!
Peely, peely, Pilka, pide,
Peely, peely, Pilka!"

Pilka barked and frisked and said:

"Yes, mistress, yes! I'll do whatever you bid me!"

Ilona gave the little dog an embroidered square of gold and silver which she herself had worked down in the Sea King's palace.

"Take this," she said to Pilka, "and put it on the pillow where the King's Son lies asleep. Perhaps when he sees it he will know that it comes from Osmo's true sister and that the frightful creature he has married is Suyettar. Then perhaps he will release Osmo before the serpents devour him. Go now, my faithful Pilka, and come back to me before the dawn."

So Pilka raced off to the King's palace carrying the square of embroidery in her teeth. Ilona waited and half an hour before sunrise the little dog came panting back.

"What news, Pilka? How fares my brother and how is my poor love, the King's Son?"

"Osmo is still with the serpents," Pilka answered, "but they haven't eaten him yet. I left the embroidered square on the pillow where the King's Son's head was lying. Suyettar was asleep on the bed beside him where you should be, dear mistress. Suyettar's awful mouth was open and she was snoring horribly. The King's Son moved uneasily for he was troubled even in his sleep."

"And did you go through the castle, Pilka?"

"Yes, dear mistress."

"And did you see the remains of the wedding feast?"

"Yes, dear mistress, the remains of a feast that shamed the King's Son, for Suyettar served bones instead of meat, fish heads, turnip tops, and bread burned to a cinder."

"Good Pilka!" Ilona said. "Good little dog! You have done well! Now the dawn is coming and I must go back to the Sea King's palace. But I shall come again to-night and also to-morrow night and do you be here waiting for me."

Pilka promised and Ilona sank down into the sea to a clanking of chains that sounded like silver bells. The King's Son heard them in his sleep and for a moment woke and said:

"What's that?"

"What's what?" snarled Suyettar. "You're dreaming! Go back to sleep!"

A few hours later when he woke again, he found the lovely square of embroidery on his pillow.

"Who made this?" he cried.

Suyettar was busy combing her snaky locks. She turned on him quickly.

"Who made what?"

When she saw the embroidery she tried to snatch it from him, but he held it tight.

"I made it, of course!" she declared. "Who but me would sit up all night and work while you lay snoring!"

But the King's Son, as he folded the embroidery, muttered to himself:

"It doesn't look to me much like your work!"

After he had breakfasted, the King's Son asked for news of Osmo. A slave was sent to the place of the serpents and when he returned he reported that Osmo was sitting amongst them uninjured.

"The old king snake has made friends with him," he added, "and has wound himself around Osmo's arm."

The King's Son was amazed at this news and also relieved, for the whole affair troubled him sorely and he was beginning to suspect a mystery.

He knew an old wise woman who lived alone in a little hut on the seashore and he decided he would go and consult her. So he went to her and told her about Osmo and how Osmo had deceived him in regard to his sister. Then he told her how the serpents instead of devouring Osmo had made friends with him and last he showed her the square of lovely embroidery he had found on his pillow that morning.

"There is a mystery somewhere, granny," he said in conclusion, "and I know not how to solve it."

The old woman looked at him thoughtfully.

"My son," she said at last, "that is never Osmo's sister that you have married. Take an old woman's word—it is Suyettar! Yet Osmo's sister must be alive and the embroidery must be a token from her. It probably means that she begs you to release her brother."

"Suyettar!" repeated the King's Son, aghast.

At first he couldn't believe such a horrible thing possible and yet that, if it were so, would explain much.

"I wonder if you're right," he said. "I must be on my guard!"

That night on the stroke of midnight to the sound of silver chimes Ilona came floating up through the waves and little Pilka, as she appeared, greeted her with barks of joy.

As before Ilona sang:

> "Peely, peely, Pilka, pide,
> Lift the latch and slip inside!
> Past the watchdog in the yard,
> Past the sleeping men on guard!
> Creep in softly as a snake,
> Then creep out before they wake!
> Peely, peely, Pilka, pide,
> Peely, peely, Pilka!"

This time Ilona gave Pilka a shirt for the King's Son. Beautifully embroidered it was in gold and silver and Ilona herself had worked it in the Sea King's palace.

Pilka carried it safely to the castle and left it on the pillow where the King's Son could see it as soon as he woke. Then Pilka visited the place of the serpents and before the first ray of dawn was back at the seashore to reassure Ilona of Osmo's safety.

Then dawn came and Ilona, as she sank in the waves to the chime of silver bells, called out to Pilka:

"Meet me here to-night at the same hour! Fail me not, dear Pilka, for to-night is the last night that the Sea King will allow me to come to the upper world!"

Pilka, howling with grief, made promise:

"I'll be here, dear mistress, that I will!"

The King's Son that morning, as he opened his eyes, saw the embroidered shirt lying on the pillow at his head. He thought at first he must be dreaming for it was more beautiful than any shirt that had ever been worked by human fingers.

"Ah!" he sighed at last, "who made this?"

"Who made what?" Suyettar demanded rudely.

When she saw the shirt she tried to snatch it, but the King's Son held it from her. Then she pretended to laugh and said:

"Oh, that! I made it, of course! Do you think any one else in the world would sit up all night and work for you while you lie there snoring! And small thanks I get for it, too!"

"It doesn't look to me like your work!" said the King's Son significantly.

Again the slave reported to him that Osmo was alive and unhurt by the serpents.

"Strange!" thought the King's Son.

He took the embroidered shirt and made the old wise woman another visit.

"Ah!" she said, when she saw the shirt, "now I understand! Listen, my Prince: last night at midnight I was awakened by the chime of silver bells and I got up and looked out the door. Just there at the water's edge, close to that little boat, I saw a strange sight. A lovely maiden rose from the waves holding in her hands the very shirt that you now have. A little dog that was lying in the boat greeted her with barks of joy. She sang a magic rime to the dog and gave it the shirt and off it ran. That maid, my Prince, must be Ilona. She must be in the Sea King's power and I think she is begging you to rescue her and to release her brother."

The King's Son slowly nodded his head.

"Granny, I'm sure what you say is true! Help me to rescue Ilona and I shall reward you richly."

"Then, my son, you must act at once, for to-night, I heard Ilona say, is the last night that the Sea King will allow her to come to the upper world. Go now to the smith and have him forge you a strong iron chain and a great strong scythe. Then to-night hide you down yonder in the shadow of the boat. At midnight when you hear the silver chimes and the maiden slowly rises from the waves, throw the iron chain about her and quickly draw her to you. Then, with one sweep of your scythe, cut the silver chains that are fastened to her ankles. But remember, my son, that is not all. She is under enchantment and as you try to grasp her the Sea King will change her to many things—a fish, a bird, a fly, and I know not what, and if in any form she escape you, then all is lost."

At once the King's Son hurried away to the smithy and had the smith forge him a strong iron chain and a heavy sharp scythe. Then when night fell he hid in the shadow of the boat and waited. Pilka snuggled up beside him. Midnight came and to the sweet chiming as of silver bells Ilona slowly rose from the waves. As she came she began singing:

"Peely, peely, Pilka, pide—"

Instantly the King's Son threw the strong iron chain about her and drew her to him. Then with one mighty sweep of the scythe he severed the silver chains that were attached to her ankles and the silver chains fell chiming into the depths. Another instant and the maiden in his arms was no maiden but a slimy fish that squirmed and wriggled and almost slipped through his fingers. He killed the fish and, lo! it was not a fish but a frightened bird that struggled to escape. He killed the bird and, lo! it was not a bird but a writhing lizard. And so on through many transformations, growing finally small and weak until at last there was only a mosquito. He crushed this and in his arms he found again the lovely Ilona.

"Ah, dear one," he said, "you are my true bride and not Suyettar who pretended she was you! Come, we will go at once to the castle and confront her!"

But Ilona cried out at this:

"Not there, my Prince, not there! Suyettar if she saw me would kill me and devour me! Keep me from her!"

"Very well, my dear one," the King's Son said. "We'll wait until to-morrow and after to-morrow there will be no Suyettar to fear."

So for that night they took shelter in the old wise woman's hut, Ilona and the King's Son and faithful little Pilka.

The next morning early the King's Son returned to the castle and had the *sauna* heated. Just inside the door he had a deep hole dug and filled it with burning tar. Then over the top of the hole he stretched a brown mat and on the brown mat a blue mat. When all was ready he went indoors and roused Suyettar.

"Where have you been all night?" she demanded angrily.

"Forgive me this time," he begged in pretended humility, "and I promise never again to be parted from my own true bride. Come now, my dear, and bathe for the *sauna* is ready."

Then Suyettar, who loved to have people see her go to the *sauna* just as if she were a real human being, put on a long bathrobe and clapped her hands. Four slaves appeared. Two took up the train of her bathrobe and the two others supported her on either side. Slowly she marched out of the castle, across the courtyard, and over to the *sauna*.

"They all really think I'm a human princess!" she said to herself, and she was so sure she was beautiful and admired that she tossed her head and smirked from side to side and took little mincing steps.

When she reached the *sauna* she was ready to drop the bathrobe and jump over the doorsill to the steaming shelf, but the King's Son whispered:

"Nay! Nay! Remember your dignity as a beautiful princess and walk over the blue mat!"

So with one more toss of her head, one more smirk of her ugly face, Suyettar stepped on the blue mat and sank into the hole of burning tar. Then the King's Son quickly locked the door of the *sauna* and left her there to burn in the tar, for burning, you know, is the only way to destroy Suyettar. As she burned the last hateful thing Suyettar did was to tear out handfuls of her hair and scatter them broadcast in the air.

"Let these," she cried, yelling and cursing, "turn into mosquitos and worms and moths and trouble mankind forever!"

Then her yells grew fainter and at last ceased altogether and the King's Son knew that it was now safe to bring Ilona home. First, however, he had Osmo released from the place of the serpents and asked his forgiveness for the unjust punishment.

Then he and Osmo together went to the hut of the old wise woman and there with tears of happiness the brother and sister were reunited. The King's Son to show his gratitude to the old wise woman begged her to accompany them to the castle and presently they all set forth with Pilka frisking ahead and barking for joy.

That day there was a new wedding feast spread at the castle and this time it was not bones and fish heads and burnt crusts but such food as the King's Son had not tasted for many a day. To celebrate his happy marriage the King's Son made Osmo his chamberlain and gave Pilka a beautiful new collar.

"Now at last," Ilona said, "I am glad I left the house of my forefathers."

THE GIANT WHO HAD NO HEART

♦

Norway

There was once upon a time a king who had seven sons. He loved them all so much that he could never do without them all at once; one had always to be with him. When they were grown up, six of them set out to woo. But the father kept the youngest son at home, and for him the others were to bring back a princess to the palace. The king gave the six the finest clothes you ever set your eyes upon, and you could see the glitter of them a long way off, and each had his own horse, which cost many, many hundred dollars, and so they set out on the journey.

After having been to many royal palaces and seen all the princesses there, they came at last to a king who had six daughters; such lovely princesses they had never seen, and so each of them began wooing one of the six sisters, and when they had got them for sweethearts, they set out for home again; but they quite forgot to bring a princess with them for Ashiepattle,[1] who was left at home, so busy were they making love to their sweethearts.

When they had journeyed a good bit of the way, they passed close to the side of a steep mountain, where there was a giant's castle. As soon as the giant saw them, he came out and turned them all, princes and princesses, into stone. But the king waited and waited for his six sons, but no sons came. He was very sad,

---

1.   The favourite hero of most Norwegian fairy tales is called "Askeladen," a sort of a male "Cinderella," and is always the youngest son of the family.

and said that he should never be glad again. "Had you not been left to me," he said to Ashiepattle, "I should not care to live any longer. I am so sad because I have lost your brothers."—"But I have been thinking to ask for leave to set out and find them, I have," said Ashiepattle.—"No, I cannot let you go," said his father; "I shall lose you as well." But Ashiepattle would go, and he begged and prayed till the king gave him leave to go. The king had no other horse to give him but an old jade, for his six brothers and their men had taken all the other horses, but Ashiepattle did not mind that; he mounted the shabby old nag.

"Good-bye, father," said he to the king, "I shall come back, sure enough, and who knows but I shall have my six brothers with me as well," and off he started.

Well, when he had got a bit on his way, he came to a raven, which was lying in the road flapping his wings, and was unable to get out of his way, it was so famished. "Oh, dear friend, give me something to eat, and I will help you in your utmost need," said the raven.—"Very little food have I," said the prince, "and you don't look as if you could help me much either, but a little I must give you, for you want it badly, I see," and then he gave the raven some of the food he had with him. When he had travelled some distance further, he came to a stream. There he saw a big salmon, which had got ashore and was dashing and knocking himself about and could not get into the water again. "Oh, dear friend! help me into the water again," said the salmon to the prince, "and I will help you in your utmost need."—"I don't suppose it can be much of a help you can give me," said the prince, "but it is a pity you should lie there and very likely perish," so he shoved the fish into the stream again. So he travelled a long, long way, till he met a wolf, which was so famished that he was only able to drag himself along the road. "Dear friend, give me your horse," said the wolf. "I am so hungry, I hear the wind whistling in my empty stomach. I have had nothing to eat for two years."—"No," said Ashiepattle, "I can't do it; first I came to a raven which I had to give all my food to; then I came to a salmon which I had to help back into the water; and now you want my horse. But that is impossible, for then I should have nothing to ride upon."—"Yes, yes, my friend, but you must help me," said the wolf, "you can ride on me instead; I shall help you again in your utmost need."—"Well, the help you can give me will not be great; but I suppose you must have the horse then, since you are so needy," said the prince. And when the wolf had finished the horse Ashiepattle took the bridle and put the bit in the wolf's mouth and the saddle on his back, and the wolf felt now so strong and well after what he had had to eat, that he set off with the prince as if he were nothing at all; Ashiepattle had never ridden so fast before. "When we get a little bit further I will show you a giant's castle," said the wolf, and in a little while they came there. "See, here is the giant's castle," said the wolf again, "and there you see all your six brothers, whom the giant has turned into stone, and there are their six brides. Over yonder is the door of the castle, and you must go in there."—"I dare not," said the prince, "the giant will kill me."—"Not at all," answered the wolf; "when you go in there you will meet a princess. She will tell you what to do to make an end of the giant. Only do as she tells you." Well, Ashiepattle went into the castle, but to tell the truth he felt rather afraid. When he got inside, he found the giant was out; but in a chamber sat the princess, just as the wolf had said. Such a lovely maiden Ashiepattle had never seen before.

"Good heavens! what has brought you here?" said the princess, as soon as she saw him. "It's sure to be your death; no one can kill the giant who lives here, for he hasn't got any heart."—"But now when I am here, I suppose I had better try my strength with him," said Ashiepattle, "and I must see if I can't release my brothers who are standing outside here, turned into stone, and I will try to save you as well."—"Well, since you will stop, we must try and do the best we can," said the princess. "You must creep under the bed over there and listen well to what he says when I speak with him, and be sure to lie as quiet as you can."

So Ashiepattle crept under the bed, and no sooner had he done so than the giant came home. "Ugh, what a smell of Christian blood there is here," shouted the giant.—"Yes, a magpie flew over the house with a man's bone and let it fall down the chimney," said the princess; "I made haste to throw it out, but the smell doesn't go away so soon." So the giant said no more about it, and when evening came, they went to bed. When they had lain a while, the princess said: "There is one thing I wanted so very much to ask you about, if I only dared."— "Well, what can that be?" asked the giant.—"I should so like to know where your heart is, since you don't carry it about you," said the princess.—"Oh, that's a thing you needn't know anything about," said the giant, "but if you must know, it's under the stone slab in front of the door."—"Ah, ha! we shall soon see if we can't find that," said Ashiepattle to himself under the bed.

Next morning the giant got up very early and set out for the wood, but no sooner was he out of sight than Ashiepattle and the princess commenced looking for the heart under the door-slab, but although they dug and searched all they could, they could not find anything. "He has made a fool of me this time," said the princess; "but I must try him again." So she picked all the prettiest flowers she could find and strewed them over the door-slab, which they put in its right place again. When the time came for the giant to return home, Ashiepattle crept under the bed, and he had scarcely got well under before the giant came in. "Ugh, what a smell of Christian blood there is here," screamed the giant.—"Yes, a magpie flew over the house and dropped a man's bone down the chimney," said the princess; "I made haste to clear it away, but I suppose the smell hasn't gone away yet."—So the giant said no more about it, but in a little while he asked who it was that had been strewing flowers around the door-slab. "Why, I, of course," said the princess.—"And what's the meaning of it?" asked the giant.—"Well, you know I am so fond of you," said the princess, "that I couldn't help doing it when I knew that your heart was lying under there."—"Ah, indeed," said the giant, "but it isn't there after all."

When they had gone to bed in the evening, the princess asked again where his heart was, because she was so very fond of him, she said, that she would so like to know it. "Oh, it's over in the cupboard on the wall there," said the giant. Ah, ha, thought both Ashiepattle and the princess, we will soon try to find it. Next morning the giant was early out of bed, and made for the wood again, but the moment he was gone Ashiepattle and the princess were looking in the cupboard for the heart, but they looked and searched and found no heart. "Well, we must try once more," said the princess. She hung flowers and garlands around the cupboard, and when the evening came Ashiepattle crept under the bed again. Shortly the giant came in. "Ugh, Ugh!" he roared, "what a smell of Christian blood there is here."—"Yes, a magpie flew past here just now, and dropped a man's bone down the chimney," said the princess; "I made haste to throw it out, but I suppose that's what you still smell." When the giant heard this, he said no more about it; but as soon as he saw the cupboard decked out with flowers and garlands, he asked who it was that had done that. It was the princess, of course. "But what's the meaning of all this foolery?" asked the giant.—"Well, you know how fond I am of you," said the princess; "I couldn't help doing it, when I knew your heart was there."—"How can you be so foolish to believe it?" said the giant.—"Well, how can I help believing it when you say so?" answered the princess.—"Oh, you are a foolish creature," said the giant, "you can never go where my heart is!"—"Ah, well," said the princess, "but I should like to know for all that where it is."—So the giant could not refuse to tell her any longer, and he said: "Far, far away in a lake lies an island,—on that island stands a church,—in that church there is a well,—in that well swims a duck,—in that duck there is an egg,—and in the egg—well, there is my heart."

Early next morning, almost before the dawn of day, the giant set out for the wood again. "Well, I suppose I had better start as well," said Ashiepattle; "I wish I only knew the way!" He said farewell to the princess for a time, and when he came outside the castle there was the wolf still waiting for him. He told the wolf what had happened inside, and that he was now going to set out for the well in the church, if he only knew the way. The wolf asked him to jump on his back,— he would try and find the way, sure enough, he said, and away they went over hills and mountains, over fields and valleys, while the wind whistled about them. When they had travelled many, many days, they came at last to the lake. The prince did not know how he should get across it; but the wolf asked him only not to be afraid, and then he plunged into the water with the prince on his back and swam across to the island. When they came to the church, they found the key for the church-door hanging high, high up on the steeple, and at first the young prince did not know how to get hold of it. "You will have to call the raven," said the wolf, which the prince did. The raven came at once, and flew up for the key, and so the prince got inside the church. When he came to the well, the duck was there sure enough. It was swimming about just as the giant had said. He commenced calling and calling, and at last he lured her up to him and caught her. But just as he was lifting her out of the water, the duck let the egg fall in the well; and Ashiepattle didn't know how to get it up again. "You had better call the salmon," said the wolf, which the prince did. The salmon came and fetched the egg from the bottom of the well. The wolf then told him to squeeze the egg, and as soon as Ashiepattle squeezed it, they heard the giant screaming. "Squeeze it once more," said the wolf, and when the prince did so, the giant screamed still more piteously, and prayed so nicely and gently for himself; he would do all the prince wished, if he only wouldn't squeeze his heart to pieces.—"Tell him, that if he will give you back again alive your six brothers and their brides, which he turned into stone, you will spare his life," said the wolf, and Ashiepattle did so.— Yes, the giant would do that at once, and he restored the six princes and the six princesses to life.—"Now, squeeze the egg to pieces," said the wolf. Ashiepattle squeezed it flat between his hands, and the giant burst.

So when Ashiepattle had got rid of the giant, he rode back again on his friend, the wolf, to the giant's castle, and there stood all his six brothers and their brides, all alive, and then Ashiepattle went into the mountain for his own bride, and they all set out for their home, the royal palace. The old king was pleased, I can tell you, when all his seven sons came back, each with his bride. "But the loveliest of the princesses is Ashiepattle's bride after all," said the king, "and he shall sit at the top of the table with her."

And then the wedding came off, and the king gave a grand feast which lasted for many a day, and if they have not done feasting by this, why they are still at it.

JACK of SJÖHOLM
and the GAN[1]-FINN

Norway

In the days of our forefathers, when there was nothing but wretched boats up in Nordland, and folks must needs buy fair winds by the sackful from the Gan-Finn, it was not safe to tack about in the open sea in wintry weather. In those days a fisherman never grew old. It was mostly womenfolk and children, and the lame and halt, who were buried ashore.

Now there was once a boat's crew from Thjöttö in Helgeland, which had put to sea, and worked its way right up to the East Lofotens.

But that winter the fish would not bite.

They lay to and waited week after week, till the month was out, and there was nothing for it but to turn home again with their fishing gear and empty boats.

But Jack of Sjöholm, who was with them, only laughed aloud, and said that, if there were no fish there, fish would certainly be found higher northwards. Surely they hadn't rowed out all this distance only to eat up all their victuals, said he.

He was quite a young chap, who had never been out fishing before. But there was some sense in what he said for all that, thought the head-fisherman.

And so they set their sails northwards.

On the next fishing-ground they fared no better than before, but they toiled away so long as their food held out.

And now they all insisted on giving it up and turning back.

---

1.   This untranslatable word is a derivative of the Icelandic *Gandr*, and means magic of the black or malefic sort.

"If there's none here, there's sure to be some still higher up towards the north," opined Jack; "and if they had gone so far, they might surely go a little further still," quoth he.

So they tempted fortune from fishing-ground to fishing-ground, till they had ventured right up to Finmark.[2] But there a storm met them, and, try as they might to find shelter under the headlands, they were obliged at last to put out into the open sea again.

There they fared worse than ever. They had a hard time of it. Again and again the prow of the boat went under the heavy rollers, instead of over them, and later on in the day the boat foundered.

There they all sat helplessly on the keel in the midst of the raging sea, and they all complained bitterly against that fellow Jack, who had tempted them on, and led them into destruction. What would now become of their wives and children? They would starve now that they had none to care for them.

When it grew dark, their hands began to stiffen, and they were carried off by the sea one by one.

And Jack heard and saw everything, down to the last shriek and the last clutch; and to the very end they never ceased reproaching him for bringing them into such misery, and bewailing their sad lot.

"I must hold on tight now," said Jack to himself, for he was better even where he was than in the sea.

And so he tightened his knees on the keel, and held on fast till he had no feeling left in either hand or foot.

In the coal-black gusty night he fancied he heard yells from one or other of the remaining boats' crews.

"They, too, have wives and children," thought he. "I wonder whether they have also a Jack to lay the blame upon!"

Now while he thus lay there and drifted and drifted, and it seemed to him to be drawing towards dawn, he suddenly felt that the boat was in the grip of a strong shoreward current; and, sure enough, Jack got at last ashore. But whichever way he looked, he saw nothing but black sea and white snow.

---

2.   The northernmost province of Norway, right within the Arctic circle.

Now as he stood there, speering and spying about him, he saw, far away, the smoke of a Finn Gamme,[3] which stood beneath a cliff, and he managed to scramble right up to it.

The Finn was so old that he could scarcely move. He was sitting in the midst of the warm ashes, and mumbling into a big sack, and neither spoke nor answered. Large yellow humble-bees were humming about all over the snow, as if it were Midsummer; and there was only a young lass there to keep the fire alight, and give the old man his food. His grandsons and grand-daughters were with the reindeer, far far away on the *Fjeld*.

Here Jack got his clothes well dried, and the rest he so much wanted. The Finn girl, Seimke, couldn't make too much of him; she fed him with reindeer milk and marrow-bones, and he lay down to sleep on silver fox-skins.

Cosy and comfortable it was in the smoke there. But as he thus lay there, 'twixt sleep and wake, it seemed to him as if many odd things were going on round about him.

There stood the Finn in the doorway talking to his reindeer, although they were far away in the mountains. He barred the wolf's way, and threatened the bear with spells; and then he opened his skin sack, so that the storm howled and piped, and there was a swirl of ashes into the hut. And when all grew quiet again, the air was thick with yellow humble-bees, which settled inside his furs, whilst he gabbled and mumbled and wagged his skull-like head.

But Jack had something else to think about besides marvelling at the old Finn. No sooner did the heaviness of slumber quit his eyes than he strolled down to his boat.

There it lay stuck fast on the beach and tilted right over like a trough, while the sea rubbed and rippled against its keel. He drew it far enough ashore to be beyond the reach of the sea-wash.

But the longer he walked around and examined it, the more it seemed to him as if folks built boats rather for the sake of letting the sea in than for the sake of keeping the sea out. The prow was little better than a hog's snout for burrowing under the water, and the planking by the keel-piece was as flat as the bottom of a

3.   The huts peculiar to the Norwegian Finns.

chest. Everything, he thought, must be arranged very differently if boats were to be really seaworthy. The prow must be raised one or two planks higher at the very least, and made both sharp and supple, so as to bend before and cut through the waves at the same time, and then a fellow would have a chance of steering a boat smartly.

He thought of this day and night. The only relaxation he had was a chat with the Finn girl of an evening.

He couldn't help remarking that this Seimke had fallen in love with him. She strolled after him wherever he went, and her eyes always became so mournful when he went down towards the sea; she understood well enough that all his thoughts were bent upon going away.

And the Finn sat and mumbled among the ashes till his fur jacket regularly steamed and smoked.

But Seimke coaxed and wheedled Jack with her brown eyes, and gave him honeyed words as fast as her tongue could wag, till she drew him right into the smoke where the old Finn couldn't hear them.

The Gan-Finn turned his head right round.

"My eyes are stupid, and the smoke makes 'em run," said he; "what has Jack got hold of there?"

"Say it is the white ptarmigan you caught in the snare," whispered she.

And Jack felt that she was huddling up against him and trembling all over.

Then she told him so softly that he thought it was his own thoughts speaking to him, that the Finn was angry and muttering mischief, and *jöjking*,[4] against the boat which Jack wanted to build. If Jack were to complete it, said she, the Gan-Finn would no longer have any sale for his fair-winds in all Nordland. And then she warned him to look to himself and never get between the Finn and the Gan-flies.

Then Jack felt that his boat might be the undoing of him. But the worse things looked, the more he tried to make the best of them.

In the grey dawn, before the Finn was up, he made his way towards the sea-shore.

---

4.   To sing songs (here magic songs), as the Finns do. Possibly derived from the Finnish verb *joikuu*, which means monotonous chanting.

But there was something very odd about the snow-hills. They were so many and so long that there was really no end to them, and he kept on trampling in deep and deeper snow and never got to the sea-shore at all. Never before had he seen the northern lights last so long into the day. They blazed and sparkled, and long tongues of fire licked and hissed after him. He was unable to find either the beach or the boat, nor had he the least idea in the world where he really was.

At last he discovered that he had gone quite astray inland instead of down to the sea. But now, when he turned round, the sea-fog came close up against him, so dense and grey that he could see neither hand nor foot before him.

By the evening he was well-nigh worn out with weariness, and was at his wits' end what to do.

Night fell, and the snowdrifts increased.

As now he sat him down on a stone and fell a brooding and pondering how he should escape with his life, a pair of snow-shoes came gliding so smoothly towards him out of the sea-fog and stood still just in front of his feet.

"As you have found me, you may as well find the way back also," said he.

So he put them on, and let the snow-shoes go their own way over hillside and steep cliff. He let not his own eyes guide him or his own feet carry him, and the swifter he went the denser the snowflakes and the driving sea-spray came up against him, and the blast very nearly blew him off the snow-shoes.

Up hill and down dale he went over all the places where he had fared during the daytime, and it sometimes seemed as if he had nothing solid beneath him at all, but was flying in the air.

Suddenly the snow-shoes stood stock still, and he was standing just outside the entrance of the Gan-Finn's hut.

There stood Seimke. She was looking for him.

"I sent my snow-shoes after thee," said she, "for I marked that the Finn had bewitched the land so that thou should'st not find the boat. Thy *life* is safe, for he has given thee shelter in his house, but it were not well for thee to see him this evening."

Then she smuggled him in, so that the Finn did not perceive it in the thick smoke, and she gave him meat and a place to rest upon.

But when he awoke in the night, he heard an odd sound, and there was a buzzing and a singing far away in the air:

> "The Finn the boat can never bind,
> The Fly the boatman cannot find,
> But round in aimless whirls doth wind."

The Finn was sitting among the ashes and *jöjking*, and muttering till the ground quite shook, while Seimke lay with her forehead to the floor and her hands clasped tightly round the back of her neck, praying against him to the Finn God. Then Jack understood that the Gan-Finn was still seeking after him amidst the snow-flakes and sea-fog, and that his life was in danger from magic spells.

So he dressed himself before it was light, went out, and came tramping in again all covered with snow, and said he had been after bears in their winter retreats. But never had he been in such a sea-fog before; he had groped about far and wide before he found his way back into the hut again, though he stood just outside it.

The Finn sat there with his skin-wrappings as full of yellow flies as a beehive. He had sent them out searching in every direction, but back they had all come, and were humming and buzzing about him.

When he saw Jack in the doorway, and perceived that the flies had pointed truly, he grew somewhat milder, and laughed till he regularly shook within his skin-wrappings, and mumbled, "The bear we'll bind fast beneath the scullery-sink, and his eyes I've turned all awry,[5] so that he can't see his boat,[6] and I'll stick a sleeping-peg in front of him till spring time."

But the same day the Finn stood in the doorway, and was busy making magic signs and strange strokes in the air.

Then he sent forth two hideous Gan-flies, which flitted off on their errands, and scorched black patches beneath them in the snow wherever they went. They were to bring pain and sickness to a cottage down in the swamps, and spread abroad the Finn disease, which was to strike down a young bride at Bodö with consumption.

But Jack thought of nothing else night and day but how he could get the better of the Gan-Finn.

---

5.   The Norse *Kverva Syni* is to delude the sight by magic spells.
6.   *I.e.*, the boat he (Jack) wanted to build.

The lass Seimke wheedled him and wept and begged him, as he valued his life, not to try to get down to his boat again. At last, however, she saw it was no use—he had made up his mind to be off.

Then she kissed his hands and wept bitterly. At least he must promise to wait till the Gan-Finn had gone right away to Jokmok[7] in Sweden.

On the day of his departure, the Finn went all round his hut with a torch and took stock. Far away as they were, there stood the mountain pastures, with the reindeer and the dogs, and the Finn's people all drew near. The Finn took the tale of the beasts, and bade his grandsons not let the reindeer stray too far while he was away, and could not guard them from wolves and bears. Then he took a sleeping potion and began to dance and turn round and round till his breath quite failed him, and he sank moaning to the ground. His furs were all that remained behind of him. His spirit had gone—gone all the way over to Jokmok.

There the magicians were all sitting together in the dark sea-fog beneath the shelter of the high mountain, and whispering about all manner of secret and hidden things, and blowing spirits into the novices of the black art.

But the Gan-flies, humming and buzzing, went round and round the empty furs of the Gan-Finn like a yellow ring and kept watch.

In the night Jack was awakened by something pulling and tugging at him as if from far away. There was as it were a current of air, and something threatened and called to him from the midst of the snowflakes outside—

"Until thou canst swim like the duck or the drake,
The egg[8] thou'dst be hatching no progress shall make;
The Finn shall ne'er let thee go southwards with sail,
For he'll screw off the wind and imprison the gale."

At the end of it the Gan-Finn was standing there, and bending right over him. The skin of his face hung down long and loose, and full of wrinkles, like an old reindeer skin, and there was a dizzying smoke in his eyes. Then Jack began to shiver and stiffen in all his limbs, and he knew that the Finn was bent upon bewitching him.

---

7. A mountain between Sweden and Norway.
8. *I.e.*, the boat he would be building.

Then he set his face rigidly against it, so that the magic spells should not get at him; and thus they struggled with one another till the Gan-Finn grew green in the face, and was very near choking.

After that the sorcerers of Jokmok sent magic shots after Jack, and clouded his wits. He felt so odd; and whenever he was busy with his boat, and had put something to rights in it, something else would immediately go wrong, till at last he felt as if his head were full of pins and needles.

Then deep sorrow fell upon him. Try as he would, he couldn't put his boat together as he would have it; and it looked very much as if he would never be able to cross the sea again.

But in the summer time Jack and Seimke sat together on the headland in the warm evenings, and the gnats buzzed and the fishes spouted close ashore in the stillness, and the eider-duck swam about.

"If only some one would build me a boat as swift and nimble as a fish, and able to ride upon the billows like a sea-mew!" sighed and lamented Jack, "then I could be off."

"Would you like me to guide you to Thjöttö?" said a voice up from the sea-shore.

There stood a fellow in a flat turned-down skin cap, whose face they couldn't see.

And right outside the boulders there, just where they had seen the eider-duck, lay a long and narrow boat, with high prow and stern; and the tar-boards were mirrored plainly in the clear water below; there was not so much as a single knot in the wood.

"I would be thankful for any such guidance," said Jack.

When Seimke heard this, she began to cry and take on terribly. She fell upon his neck, and wouldn't let go, and raved and shrieked. She promised him her snow-shoes, which would carry him through everything, and said she would steal for him the bone-stick from the Gan-Finn, so that he might find all the old lucky dollars that ever were buried, and would teach him how to make salmon-catching knots in the fishing lines, and how to entice the reindeer from afar. He should become as rich as the Gan-Finn, if only he wouldn't forsake her.

But Jack had only eyes for the boat down there. Then she sprang up, and tore down her black locks, and bound them round his feet, so that he had to wrench them off before he could get quit of her.

"If I stay here and play with you and the young reindeer, many a poor fellow will have to cling with broken nails to the keel of a boat,"[9] said he. "If you like to make it up, give me a kiss and a parting hug, or shall I go without them?"

Then she threw herself into his arms like a young wild cat, and looked straight into his eyes through her tears, and shivered and laughed, and was quite beside herself.

But when she saw she could do nothing with him, she rushed away, and waved her hands above her head in the direction of the Gamme.[10]

Then Jack understood that she was going to take counsel of the Gan-Finn, and that he had better take refuge in his boat before the way was closed to him. And, in fact, the boat had come so close up to the boulders, that he had only to step down upon the thwarts. The rudder glided into his hand, and aslant behind the mast sat some one at the prow, and hoisted and stretched the sail: but his face Jack could not see.

Away they went.

And such a boat for running before the wind Jack had never seen before. The sea stood up round about them like a deep snow-drift, although it was almost calm. But they hadn't gone very far before a nasty piping began in the air. The birds shrieked and made for land, and the sea rose like a black wall behind them.

It was the Gan-Finn who had opened his wind-sack, and sent a storm after them.

"One needs a full sail in the Finn-cauldron here," said something from behind the mast.

The fellow who had the boat in hand took such little heed of the weather that he did not so much as take in a single clew.

Then the Gan-Finn sent double knots[11] after them.

They sped along in a wild dance right over the firth, and the sea whirled up in white columns of foam, reaching to the very clouds.

---

9. Meaning that he would never have a chance of building the new sort of boat that his mind was bent on.
10. The Finn's hut.
11. *Tvinde Knuder.* When the Finn tied *one* magic knot, he raised a gale, so two knots would give a tempest.

Unless the boat could fly as quick and quicker than a bird, it was lost.

Then a hideous laugh was heard to larboard—

"Anfinn Ganfinn gives mouth,

And blows us right south;

There's a crack[12] in the sack,

With three clews we must tack."

And heeling right over, with three clews in the sail, and the heavy foremost fellow astride on the sheer-strake, with his huge sea-boots dangling in the sea-foam, away they scudded through the blinding spray right into the open sea, amidst the howling and roaring of the wind.

The billowy walls were so vast and heavy that Jack couldn't even see the light of day across the yards, nor could he exactly make out whether they were going under or over the sea-trough.

The boat shook the sea aside as lightly and easily as if its prow were the slippery fin of a fish, and its planking was as smooth and fine as the shell of a tern's egg; but, look as he would, Jack couldn't see where these planks ended; it was just as if there was only half a boat and no more; and at last it seemed to him as if the whole of the front part came off in the sea-foam, and they were scudding along under sail in half a boat.

When night fell, they went through the sea-fire, which glowed like hot embers, and there was a prolonged and hideous howling up in the air to windward.

And cries of distress and howls of mortal agony answered the wind from all the upturned boat keels they sped by, and many hideously pale-looking folks clutched hold of their thwarts. The gleam of the sea-fire cast a blue glare on their faces, and they sat, and gaped, and glared, and yelled at the blast.

Suddenly he awoke, and something cried, "Now thou art at home at Thjöttö, Jack!"

And when he had come to himself a bit, he recognized where he was. He was lying over against the boulders near his boathouse at home. The tide had come so far inland that a border of foam gleamed right up in the potato-field, and he could scarcely keep his feet for the blast. He sat him down in the boathouse, and began

---

12. *I.e.*, where the Gan-Finn let out the wind.

scratching and marking out the shape of the Draugboat in the black darkness till sleep overtook him.

When it was light in the morning, his sister came down to him with a meat-basket. She didn't greet him as if he were a stranger, but behaved as if it were the usual thing for her to come thus every morning. But when he began telling her all about his voyage to Finmark, and the Gan-Finn, and the Draugboat he had come home in at night, he perceived that she only grinned and let him chatter. And all that day he talked about it to his sister and his brothers and his mother, until he arrived at the conclusion that they thought him a little out of his wits. When he mentioned the Draugboat they smiled amongst themselves, and evidently went out of their way to humour him. But they might believe what they liked, if only he could carry out what he wanted to do, and be left to himself in the out-of-the-way old boathouse.

"One should go with the stream," thought Jack; and if they thought him crazy and out of his wits, he ought to behave so that they might beware of interfering with him, and disturbing him in his work.

So he took a bed of skins with him down to the boathouse, and slept there at night; but in the daytime he perched himself on a pole on the roof, and bellowed out that now he was sailing. Sometimes he rode astraddle on the roof ridge, and dug his sheath-knife deep into the rafters, so that people might think he fancied himself at sea, holding fast on to the keel of a boat.

Whenever folks passed by, he stood in the doorway, and turned up the whites of his eyes so hideously, that everyone who saw him was quite scared. As for the people at home, it was as much as they dared to stick his meat-basket into the boathouse for him. So they sent it to him by his youngest sister, merry little Malfri, who would sit and talk with him, and thought it such fun when he made toys and playthings for her, and talked about the boat which should go like a bird, and sail as no other boat had ever sailed.

If any one chanced to come upon him unexpectedly, and tried to peep and see what he was about in the boathouse there, he would creep up into the timber-loft and bang and pitch the boards and planks about, so that they didn't know exactly where to find him, and were glad enough to be off. But one and all made haste to climb over the hill again when they heard him fling himself down at full length and send peal after peal of laughter after them.

So that was how Jack got folks to leave him at peace.

He worked best at night when the storm tore and tugged at the stones and birchbark of the turf roof, and the sea-wrack came right up to the boathouse door.

When it piped and whined through the fissured walls, and the fine snowflakes flitted through the cracks, the model of the Draugboat stood plainest before him. The winter days were short, and the wick of the train-oil lamp, which hung over him as he worked, cast deep shadows, so that the darkness came soon and lasted a long way into the morning, when he sought sleep in his bed of skins with a heap of shavings for his pillow.

He spared no pains or trouble. If there was a board which would not run into the right groove with the others, though never so little, he would take out a whole row of them and plane them all round again and again.

Now, one night, just before Christmas, he had finished all but the uppermost planking and the gabs. He was working so hard to finish up that he took no count of time.

The plane was sending the shavings flying their briskest when he came to a dead stop at something black which was moving along the plank.

It was a large and hideous fly which was crawling about and feeling and poking all the planks in the boat. When it reached the lowest keel-board it whirred with its wings and buzzed. Then it rose and swept above it in the air till, all at once, it swerved away into the darkness.

Jack's heart sank within him. Such doubt and anguish came upon him. He knew well enough that no good errand had brought the Gan-fly buzzing over the boat like that.

So he took the train-oil lamp and a wooden club, and began to test the prow and light up the boarding, and thump it well, and go over the planks one by one. And in this way he went over every bit of the boat from stem to stern, both above and below. There was not a nail or a rivet that he really believed in now.

But now neither the shape nor the proportions of the boat pleased him anymore. The prow was too big, and the whole cut of the boat all the way down the gunwale had something of a twist and a bend and a swerve about it, so that it looked like the halves of two different boats put together, and the half in front didn't fit in with the half behind. As he was about to look into the matter still further (and he felt the cold sweat bursting out of the roots of his hair), the train-oil lamp went out and left him in blank darkness.

Then he could contain himself no longer. He lifted his club and burst open the boathouse door, and, snatching up a big cow-bell, he began to swing it about him and ring and ring with it through the black night.

"Art chiming for me, Jack?" something asked. There was a sound behind him like the surf sucking at the shore, and a cold blast blew into the boathouse.

There on the keel-stick sat some one in a sloppy grey sea-jacket, and with a print cap drawn down over its ears, so that its skull looked like a low tassel.

Jack gave a great start. This was the very being he had been thinking of in his wild rage. Then he took the large bailing can and flung it at the Draug.

But right through the Draug it went, and rattled against the wall behind, and back again it came whizzing about Jack's ears, and if it had struck him he would never have got up again.

The old fellow, however, only blinked his eyes a little savagely.

"Fie!" cried Jack, and spat at the uncanny thing—and back into his face again he got as good as he gave.

"There you have your wet clout back again!" cried a laughing voice.

But the same instant Jack's eyes were opened and he saw a whole boat-building establishment on the sea-shore.

And, there, ready and rigged out on the bright water, lay an Ottring,[13] so long and shapely and shining that his eyes could not feast on it enough.

The old 'un blinked with satisfaction. His eyes became more and more glowing.

"If I could guide you back to Helgeland," said he, "I could put you in the way of gaining your bread too. But you must pay me a little tax for it. In every seventh boat you build 'tis I who must put in the keel-board."

Jack felt as if he were choking. He felt that the boat was dragging him into the very jaws of an abomination.

---

13.   An eight-oared boat.

"Or do you fancy you'll worm the trick out of me for nothing?" said the gaping grinning Draug.

Then there was a whirring sound, as if something heavy was hovering about the boathouse, and there was a laugh: "If you want the *seaman's* boat you must take the *dead man's* boat along with it. If you knock three times to-night on the keel-piece with the club, you shall have such help in building boats that the like of them will not be found in all Nordland."

Twice did Jack raise his club that night, and twice he laid it aside again.

But the *Ottring* lay and frisked and sported in the sea before his eyes, just as he had seen it, all bright and new with fresh tar, and with the ropes and fishing gear just put in. He kicked and shook the fine slim boat with his foot just to see how light and high she could rise on the waves above the water-line.

And once, twice, thrice, the club smote against the keel-piece.

So that was how the first boat was built at Sjöholm.

Thick as birds together stood a countless number of people on the headland in the autumn, watching Jack and his brothers putting out in the new *Ottring*.

It glided through the strong current so that the foam was like a foss all round it.

Now it was gone, and now it ducked up again like a sea-mew, and past skerries and capes it whizzed like a dart.

Out in the fishing grounds the folks rested upon their oars and gaped. Such a boat they had never seen before.

But if in the first year it was an *Ottring,* next year it was a broad heavy *Femböring* for winter fishing which made the folks open their eyes.

And every boat that Jack turned out was lighter to row and swifter to sail than the one before it.

But the largest and finest of all was the last that stood on the stocks on the shore.

This was the *seventh*.

Jack walked to and fro, and thought about it a good deal; but when he came down to see it in the morning, it seemed to him, oddly enough, to have grown in the night and, what is more, was such a wondrous beauty that he was struck dumb with astonishment. There it lay ready at last, and folks were never tired of talking about it.

Now, the Bailiff who ruled over all Helgeland in those days was an unjust man who laid heavy taxes upon the people, taking double weight and tale both of fish and of eider-down, nor was he less grasping with the tithes and grain dues. Wherever his fellows came they fleeced and flayed. No sooner, then, did the rumour of the new boats reach him than he sent his people out to see what truth was in it, for he himself used to go fishing in the fishing grounds with large crews. When thus his fellows came back and told him what they had seen, the Bailiff was so taken with it that he drove straightway over to Sjöholm, and one fine day down he came swooping on Jack like a hawk. "Neither tithe nor tax hast thou paid for thy livelihood, so now thou shalt be fined as many half-marks of silver as thou hast made boats," said he.

Ever louder and fiercer grew his rage. Jack should be put in chains and irons and be transported northwards to the fortress of Skraar, and be kept so close that he should never see sun or moon more.

But when the Bailiff had rowed round the *Femböring*, and feasted his eyes upon it, and seen how smart and shapely it was, he agreed at last to let Mercy go before Justice, and was content to take the *Femböring* in lieu of a fine.

Then Jack took off his cap and said that if there was one man more than another to whom he would like to give the boat, it was his honour the Bailiff.

So off the magistrate sailed with it.

Jack's mother and sister and brothers cried bitterly at the loss of the beautiful *Femböring*; but Jack stood on the roof of the boat-house and laughed fit to split.

And towards autumn the news spread that the Bailiff with his eight men had gone down with the *Femböring* in the West-fjord.

But in those days there was quite a changing about of boats all over Nordland, and Jack was unable to build a tenth part of the boats required of him. Folks from near and far hung about the walls of his boat-house, and it was quite a favour on his part to take orders, and agree to carry them out. A whole score of boats soon stood beneath the pent-house on the strand.

He no longer troubled his head about every *seventh* boat, or cared to know which it was or what befell it. If a boat foundered now and then, so many the more got off and did well, so that, on the whole, he made a very good thing indeed out of it. Besides, surely folks could pick and choose their own boats, and take which they liked best.

But Jack got so great and mighty that it was not advisable for any one to thwart him, or interfere where he ruled and reigned.

Whole rows of silver dollars stood in the barrels in the loft, and his boat-building establishment stretched over all the islands of Sjöholm.

One Sunday his brothers and merry little Malfri had gone to church in the *Femböring*. When evening came, and they hadn't come home, the boatman came in and said that some one had better sail out and look after them, as a gale was blowing up.

Jack was sitting with a plumb-line in his hand, taking the measurements of a new boat, which was to be bigger and statelier than any of the others, so that it was not well to disturb him.

"Do you fancy they're gone out in a rotten old tub, then?" bellowed he. And the boatman was driven out as quickly as he had come.

But at night Jack lay awake and listened. The wind whined outside and shook the walls, and there were cries from the sea far away. And just then there came a knocking at the door, and some one called him by name.

"Go back whence you came," cried he, and nestled more snugly in his bed.

Shortly afterwards there came the fumbling and the scratching of tiny fingers at the door.

"Can't you leave me at peace o' nights?" he bawled, "or must I build me another bedroom?"

But the knocking and the fumbling for the latch outside continued, and there was a sweeping sound at the door, as of some one who could not open it. And there was a stretching of hands towards the latch ever higher and higher.

But Jack only lay there and laughed. "The *Fembörings* that are built at Sjöholm don't go down before the first blast that blows," mocked he.

Then the latch chopped and hopped till the door flew wide open, and in the doorway stood pretty Malfri and her mother and brothers. The sea-fire shone about them, and they were dripping with water.

Their faces were pale and blue, and pinched about the corners of the mouth, as if they had just gone through their death agony. Malfri had one stiff arm round her mother's neck; it was all torn and bleeding, just as when she had gripped her for the last time. She railed and lamented, and begged back her young life from him.

So now he knew what had befallen them.

Out into the dark night and the darker weather he went straightway to search for them, with as many boats and folk as he could get together. They sailed and searched in every direction, and it was in vain.

But towards day the *Femböring* came drifting homewards bottom upwards, and with a large hole in the keel-board.

Then he knew who had done the deed.

But since the night when the whole of Jack's family went down, things were very different at Sjöholm.

In the daytime, so long as the hammering and the banging and the planing and the clinching rang about his ears, things went along swimmingly, and the frames of boat after boat rose thick as sea fowl on an *Æggevær*.[14]

But no sooner was it quiet of an evening than he had company. His mother bustled and banged about the house, and opened and shut drawers and cupboards, and the stairs creaked with the heavy tread of his brothers going up to their bedrooms.

At night no sleep visited his eyes, and sure enough pretty Malfri came to his door and sighed and groaned.

Then he would lie awake there and think, and reckon up how many boats with false keel-boards he might have sent to sea. And the longer he reckoned the more draug-boats he made of it.

Then he would plump out of bed and creep through the dark night down to the boathouse. There he held a light beneath the boats, and banged and tested all the keel-boards with a club to see if he couldn't hit upon the *seventh*. But he neither heard nor felt a single board give way. One was just like another. They were all hard and supple, and the wood, when he scraped off the tar, was white and fresh.

One night he was so tormented by an uneasiness about the new *Sekstring*,[15]

14. A place where sea-birds' eggs abound.
15. A contraction of *Sexæring*, *i.e.*, a boat with six oars.

which lay down by the bridge ready to set off next morning, that he had no peace till he went down and tested its keel-board with his club.

But while he sat in the boat, and was bending over the thwart with a light, there was a gulping sound out at sea, and then came such a vile stench of rottenness. The same instant he heard a wading sound, as of many people coming ashore, and then up over the headland he saw a boat's crew coming along.

They were all crooked-looking creatures, and they all leaned right forward and stretched out their arms before them. Whatever came in their way, both stone and stour,[16] they went right through it, and there was neither sound nor shriek.

Behind them came another boat's crew, big and little, grown men and little children, rattling and creaking.

And crew after crew came ashore and took the path leading to the headland.

When the moon peeped forth Jack could see right into their skeletons. Their faces glared, and their mouths gaped open with glistening teeth, as if they had been swallowing water. They came in heaps and shoals, one after the other: the place quite swarmed with them.

Then Jack perceived that here were all they whom he had tried to count and reckon up as he lay in bed, and a fit of fury came upon him.

He rose in the boat and spanked his leather breeches behind and cried: "You would have been even more than you are already if Jack hadn't built his boats!"

But now like an icy whizzing blast they all came down upon him, staring at him with their hollow eyes.

They gnashed their teeth, and each one of them sighed and groaned for his lost life.

Then Jack, in his horror, put out from Sjöholm.

But the sail slackened, and he glided into dead water.[17] There, in the midst of the still water, was a floating mass of rotten swollen planks. All of them had once been shaped and fashioned together, but were now burst and sprung, and slime and green mould and filth and nastiness hung about them.

Dead hands grabbed at the corners of them with their white knuckles and

---

16. Eng. dialect word (the Norse is *staur*) meaning impediments of any kind.
17. *Daudvatn* (Dan. *Dödvand*), water in which there is no motion.

couldn't grip fast. They stretched themselves across the water and sank again.

Then Jack let out all his clews and sailed and sailed and tacked according as the wind blew.

He glared back at the rubbish behind him to see if those *things* were after him. Down in the sea all the dead hands were writhing, and tried to strike him with gaffs astern.

Then there came a gust of wind whining and howling, and the boat drove along betwixt white seething rollers.

The weather darkened, thick snowflakes filled the air, and the rubbish around him grew greener.

In the daytime he took the cormorants far away in the grey mist for his land-marks, and at night they screeched about his ears.

And the birds flitted and flitted continually, but Jack sat still and looked out upon the hideous cormorants.

At last the sea-fog lifted a little, and the air began to be alive with bright, black, buzzing flies. The sun burned, and far away inland the snowy plains blazed in its light.

He recognized very well the headland and shore where he was now able to lay to. The smoke came from the Gamme up on the snow-hill there. In the doorway sat the Gan-Finn. He was lifting his pointed cap up and down, up and down, by means of a thread of sinew, which went right through him, so that his skin creaked.

And up there also sure enough was Seimke.

She looked old and angular as she bent over the reindeer-skin that she was spreading out in the sunny weather. But she peeped beneath her arm as quick and nimble as a cat with kittens, and the sun shone upon her, and lit up her face and pitch-black hair.

She leaped up so briskly, and shaded her eyes with her hand, and looked down at him. Her dog barked, but she quieted it so that the Gan-Finn should mark nothing.

Then a strange longing came over him, and he put ashore.

He stood beside her, and she threw her arms over her head, and laughed and shook and nestled close up to him, and cried and pleaded, and didn't know what to do with herself, and ducked down upon his bosom, and threw herself on his neck, and kissed and fondled him, and wouldn't let him go.

But the Gan-Finn had noticed that there was something amiss, and sat all the time in his furs, and mumbled and muttered to the Gan-flies, so that Jack dare not get between him and the doorway.

The Finn was angry.

Since there had been such a changing about of boats over all Nordland, and there was no more sale for his fair winds, he was quite ruined, he complained. He was now so poor that he would very soon have to go about and beg his bread. And of all his reindeer he had only a single doe left, who went about there by the house.

Then Seimke crept behind Jack, and whispered to him to bid for this doe. Then she put the reindeer-skin around her, and stood inside the Gamme door in the smoke, so that the Gan-Finn only saw the grey skin, and fancied it was the reindeer they were bringing in.

Then Jack laid his hand upon Seimke's neck, and began to bid.

The pointed cap ducked and nodded, and the Finn spat in the warm air; but sell his reindeer he would not.

Jack raised his price.

But the Finn heaved up the ashes all about him, and threatened and shrieked. The flies came as thick as snow-flakes; the Finn's furry wrappings were alive with them.

Jack bid and bid till it reached a whole bushel load of silver, and the Finn was ready to jump out of his skins.

Then he stuck his head under his furs again, and mumbled and *jöjked* till the amount rose to seven bushels of silver.

Then the Gan-Finn laughed till he nearly split. He thought the reindeer would cost the purchaser a pretty penny.

But Jack lifted Seimke up, and sprang down with her to his boat, and held the reindeer-skin behind him, against the Gan-Finn.

And they put off from land, and went to sea.

Seimke was so happy, and smote her hands together, and took her turn at the oars.

The northern light shot out like a comb, all greeny-red and fiery, and licked and played upon her face. She talked to it, and fought it with her hands, and her eyes sparkled. She used both tongue and mouth and rapid gestures as she exchanged words with it.

Then it grew dark, and she lay on his bosom, so that he could feel her warm breath. Her black hair lay right over him, and she was as soft and warm to the touch as a ptarmigan when it is frightened and its blood throbs.

Jack put the reindeer-skin over Seimke, and the boat rocked them to and fro on the heavy sea as if it were a cradle.

They sailed on and on till night-fall; they sailed on and on till they saw neither headland nor island nor sea-bird in the outer skerries more.

A NOTE ON THE SOURCES

The stories in this book were collected, translated, and published in the late nineteenth and early twentieth centuries. They have been excerpted from the following publications, all of which are in the public domain. The stories from *Yule-Tide Stories* were originally published in *Eventyr og Folkesagen fra Jylland, forfalte af Carit Etlar, Kjöb,* by Carit Etlar. The stories in *Mighty Mikko* were translated from various sources, which are not specified by the author.

Arnason, Jón, *Icelandic Legends.* Translated by George E. J. Powell and Eiríkur Magnússon. London: Richard Bentley, 1864. Internet Archive, 2009. https://archive.org/details/icelandiclegend02powegoog.

Asbjörnson, P. Ch., *Christmas Fireside Stories or Round the Yule Log: Norwegian Folk and Fairy Tales.* Translated H. L. Brækstad. London and Edinburgh: Sampson Low, Marston & Company, Limited, 1919. Internet Archive, 2007. https://archive.org/details/christmasfiresid00asbj.

Asbjörnson, P. Ch., *Tales from the Fjeld: A Series of Popular Tales from the Norse.* Translated by Sir George Dasent, D.C.L. London: Gibbings & Company Limited, New York: G.P. Putnam's Sons, 1896. Internet Archive, 2009. https://archive.org/details/cu31924079597849.

Djurklou, Baron G., *Fairy Tales from the Swedish.* Translated by H. L. Brækstad. London: William Heinemann, 1901. Internet Archive, 2008. https://archive.org/details/fairytalesfromsw00djurrich.

Fillmore, Parker, *Mighty Mikko: A Book of Finnish Fairy Tales and Folk Tales.* New York: Harcourt, Brace and Company, 1922. Internet Archive, 2007. https://archive.org/details/mightymikkobooko00fill.

Lie, Jonas, *Weird Tales from Northern Seas.* Translated by R. Nisbet Bain. London: Kegan Paul, Trench, Trubner & Co. Ltd., 1893. Internet Archive, 2008. https://archive.org/details/weirdtalesfromn00liegoog.

Yule-Tide Stories: A Collection of Scandinavian and North German Popular Tales and Traditions from the Swedish, Danish, and German. Edited by Benjamin Thorpe. London: George Bell & Sons, 1910. Internet Archive, 2007. https://archive.org/details/yuletidestoriesc00thor.

SOURCES

►◄◆►◄

"All I Possess!"
From *Fairy Tales from the Swedish*, by Baron G. Djurklou, translated by H. L. Brækstad.

The Boy Who Did Not Know What Fear Was
From *Icelandic Legends*, by Jón Arnason, translated by George E. J. Powell and Eiríkur Magnússon.

Death and the Doctor
From *Tales from the Fjeld*, by P. Ch. Asbjörnson, translated by Sir George Dasent, D.C.L.

East of the Sun and West of the Moon
From *Christmas Fireside Stories or Round the Yule Log,* by P. Ch. Asbjörnson, translated by H. L. Brækstad.

The Forest Bride
From *Mighty Mikko*, by Parker Fillmore.

The Giant Who Had No Heart
From *Christmas Fireside Stories or Round the Yule Log*, by P. Ch. Asbjörnson, translated by H. L. Brækstad.

Hildur, the Queen of the Elves
From *Icelandic Legends*, by Jón Arnason, translated by George E. J. Powell and Eiríkur Magnússon.

The Honest Penny
From *Tales of the Fjeld*, by P. Ch. Asbjörnson, translated by Sir George Dasent, D.C.L.

Jack of Sjöholm and the Gan-Finn
From *Weird Tales from Northern Seas*, by Jonas Lie, translated by R. Nisbet Bain.

The Magician's Pupil
From *Yule-Tide Stories*, edited by Benjamin Thorpe.

Mighty Mikko

From *Mighty Mikko,* by Parker Fillmore.

Old Nick and the Girl

From *Fairy Tales from the Swedish*, by Baron G. Djurklou, translated by H. L. Brækstad.

The Old Woman and the Tramp

From *Fairy Tales from the Swedish*, by Baron G. Djurklou, translated by H. L. Brækstad.

Toller's Neighbours

From *Yule-Tide Stories*, edited by Benjamin Thorpe.

The True Bride

From *Mighty Mikko,* by Parker Fillmore.

The Way of the World

From *Tales from the Fjeld,* by P. Ch. Asbjörnson, translated by Sir George Dasent, D.C.L.

The Widow's Son

From *Christmas Fireside Stories or Round the Yule Log,* by P. Ch. Asbjörnson, translated by H. L. Brækstad.